Who can learn to love a beast?

"Wh-what do you plan to do with me?"

The beast could smell the man's terror. He tried to imagine himself as this man saw him—huge, hairy paws bursting from the sleeves of his shirt, pointy ears, and beady eyes. A form built for the chase, with razor-sharp teeth made for the kill.

"You've seen my horrible face," the beast growled. "Do you think I'll let you tell the world what kind of freak I am? Tell the people in your town that a monster lives in their backyard?"

"Please, I haven't even seen you, if anyone asks. I beg you not to keep me locked up. I need to be with my daughter. I love her so much."

"What does a beast know about love?" he asked.

"Then you really won't let me go?" the man cried. "You're going to keep me locked up in here? You truly are a beast!"

"And so I am. But I'm a beast who saved your life. So humor me. Humor a lonely beast for a few days with your stories and company. You owe me that much."

"And then will you let me go?"

The fight went out of the beast. He was thirsty. So thirsty for the little details of ordinary life that this man had to offer. "Then we'll see."

Look for more books in the romantic series
Once Upon a Dream:

At Midnight: A Novel Based on Cinderella

Once Upon a Dream

The Rose

A Novel Based on
Beauty and the Beast

Jennifer Baker

SCHOLASTIC INC.
New York Toronto London Auckland Sydney

No part of this publication may be reproduced in whole or in part, or stored in a retrieval system, or transmitted in any form or by any means, electronic, mechanical, photocopying, recording, or otherwise, without written permission of the publisher. For information regarding permission, write to Scholastic Inc., 555 Broadway, New York, NY 10012.

ISBN 0-590-25948-2

Produced by Daniel Weiss Associates, Inc.
33 West 17th Street, New York, NY 10011

12 11 10 9 8 7 6 5 4 3 2 1   6 7 8 9/9 0/0

Printed in the U.S.A.   01

First Scholastic printing, January 1996

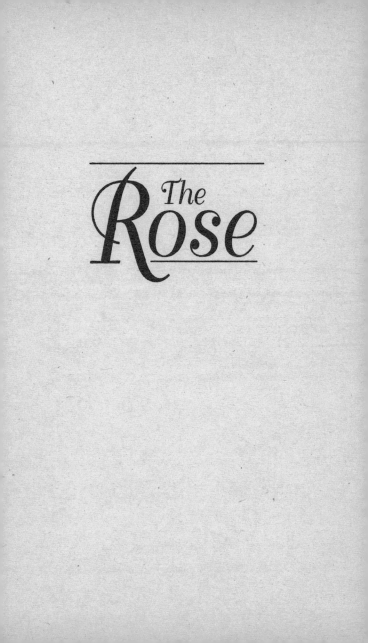

The Rose

One

Bonnie Oliviera swam across the cold bay with long, powerful strokes, the slight sting of salt water on her face refreshingly bracing. As she glided toward the shallow water, Bonnie let herself slow down. She flipped over on her back, taking deep breaths. The shimmery water rocked her gently. Overhead, silvery light filtered through a thin cover of clouds. A seagull rode the wind, giving out a nasal cry.

Bonnie stood up and waded to shore. She grabbed the towel she'd left on the shell-covered sand and wrapped it around her.

"One way to wake up," a familiar voice called out.

She looked over at the road that ran along the beach and saw Hank Lawson poking his head out the window of the town sanitation truck. His partner, Doug, was throwing a few bulging plastic sacks into the back of the truck. He tossed the last one in and then waved to her.

"Cold enough for you, Bonnie?" Doug asked.

"Just got to keep moving," she called back.

Doug climbed into the truck, and he and Hank drove off. Marnie Peoples passed them in the other direction in her rusty gray truck, probably on her way to her job at the pharmacy. She tooted her horn at Bonnie, and Bonnie waved back.

Glancing out at the water, Bonnie saw that a few boats were already heading toward the horizon. She stooped down to pull on her sneakers. "It's time to get the day started," she said out loud to herself as she headed down the beach toward the harbor.

Somewhere out there were new people and new places. Bonnie thought about the big cities down the coast that were alive in the morning rush. She imagined the people and traffic flowing through the streets like blood through veins, car horns honking, sunshine winking off the tops of skyscrapers. The elegantly dressed men and women were probably hurrying off to work, newspapers tucked under their arms, while a few late-night revelers headed home bleary-eyed. Tourists were poring over maps and sipping coffee at cafés. Schoolkids were rubbing elbows with movie stars.

Or so Bonnie liked to think. She'd only been out of Land's End County a handful of times, on school trips or the all-too-rare vacation with her father. Now she headed toward his lobster boat, docked at the far end of one of the dark, sea-soaked piers. Bonnie let the fresh sea breeze caress her face and damp hair. Here in Land's End she knew everyone, and every little turn and twist in the scattering of roads that made up the town.

"Hey, Bonnie!" called a big-bellied, gruff-voiced man. He was busily untangling nets on a squat but powerful-looking little boat. "Your dad said to tell you he went over to the Foghorn to get a cup of coffee. He's bringing you one, too."

"Thanks, Mel. How was the catch yesterday?" Bonnie called back.

Mel grimaced. "Better be better today."

Bonnie nodded. "Hope so," she said. Over the years it had gotten increasingly difficult to make a living from the sea. Pollution and overfished, underregulated waters had made for slim pickings, so Bonnie's father and Mel had to work harder each year just to stay in the same place. That was why Bonnie was working on her dad's boat now that she'd graduated from high school, instead of taking in the world outside this little town.

For a moment Bonnie pictured herself walking down a busy city street instead of the pier at the Land's End harbor. Her old bathing suit and sneakers were replaced by some chic outfit, say a creamy-colored, silky slip dress and a pair of chunky-soled mules. The faces she passed were new and different—people she'd never seen before—and every unknown street held the promise of surprise. And the promise of that special someone, whom she definitely hadn't found in Land's End.

Bonnie sighed. It wasn't only the cities down the coast she longed to visit. She dreamed of everything she'd only seen on television or read about in all the books she devoured as quickly as she could get her hands on them—the pyramids of Egypt; the Mayan ruins; the great cathedrals of Europe; the impossibly fashionable women of Milan sipping cappuccino; the Japanese executives letting down their guard at karaoke bars; the flutelike music of Guatemalan street musicians . . . and, of course, the Portuguese village where her father had been born—the old stone cottages he sometimes talked about, the richly tiled walls and rows of gleaming, multicolored bottles in the hole-in-the-wall coffee bars.

And always there would be the perfect boy to share it all with. . . .

A raspy honk brought Bonnie back to Land's End. She looked up as a brown van cruised along the road that skirted the harbor. Jan Wilson's father leaned out the driver's-side window. "Hey there, Bonnie."

"Hi, Mr. Wilson." Bonnie guessed Jan hadn't bothered to inform him that nobody was supposed to be speaking to her these days. Bonnie prepared herself to see Jan coming around the harbor bend in her red Saturn, on her way to work the breakfast shift at the Foghorn. Jan and her father usually left the house at around the same time every morning.

Bonnie thought about the last time Jan had uttered a word to her, a few months ago, at school.

Bonnie had been walking down the crowded hall with her friend Doris on her way to bio class. Up ahead of them, hanging out by the lockers, were Jan, Sue Patella, Nina Braxton—the popular kids. Gary Belsky was there, too, and Jan was flirting madly with him.

"She looks like she's about to slobber all over him right in front of everyone," Doris commented.

Bonnie shrugged. "He loves it. Feeds his oversized ego."

"Well, he *is* pretty cute," Doris allowed.

"Until you get to know him," Bonnie whispered back as they got nearer. "Hey, everyone," she said more loudly to Jan and company.

"Yo, Bonnie," Gary greeted her. "Jan was just talking about the prom and stuff. You going with anyone?" He put his arm around her suggestively. " 'Cause I'm not taken yet."

Bonnie saw Jan shoot her a murderous look. She shrugged out of Gary's hold. "I'm sure you'll find a date," she said uncomfortably.

"Hey, I wasn't worried about that," Gary answered obnoxiously.

Bonnie looped her arm through Doris's. "Good," she answered. "Well, we don't want to be late for class." She steered Doris down the hall in a hurry.

Jan caught up with them by the water fountain. "Bonnie, if you know what's good for you, you'll stay away from Gary," she warned venomously.

"He's all yours," Bonnie assured her.

"Better be," Jan shot back.

Since then, neither Jan nor any of her popular clique had as much as spoken to Bonnie, even though Gary had finally wound up at the prom with Jan.

"Ignore them. It'll blow over," Doris had advised. Easy for Doris to say. She was away for the whole summer, the lucky duck, driving cross-country with her family in their trailer. Bonnie was stuck here, in a town so little it was hard to avoid anyone for very long.

Now Bonnie watched Jan's father drive off. Sure enough, Jan's red car came into sight only seconds later, going way too fast for a narrow, sandy road. Jan sped by without any indication that she'd seen Bonnie. She passed the playground and squealed into the Foghorn's parking lot.

And now, Bonnie thought, *Mel will say*—

"Where'd she get her driver's license? The local department store?"

Yep. Everyone knew everyone, and everything, backward and forward in this town. Not too many surprises—even when you were a wash-ashore.

Bonnie laughed to herself. A wash-ashore. That's what they called it around here when you weren't from these parts. She'd spent her whole life in this town—she only *dreamed* of knowing something else—but because her father had been born in a foreign country, because he still spoke with the faint accent of his native Portuguese, they were wash-ashores.

Bonnie's mother's family was Land's End for generations back—like so many of the people here. One of the roads outside of town bore her maiden name, and in the old part of the cemetery a whole section of cracked, weathered headstones marked Bonnie's ancestors on her mother's side. Bonnie had inherited her mother's toffee-colored hair and delicate features, but since her mother had died when Bonnie was born, it was her father from whom she'd inherited her status in town.

Bonnie reached the end of the dock and nimbly hopped onto the *Bonita II*. Of course, her dad's wacky inventions didn't exactly make him fit in around here, either. She shot a dubious look at the boat's intricate system of pulleys and hoses and buckets—a system her father had designed to haul the lobster traps out of the water, then clean and rebait them at the same time. The week before, the whole thing had freaked out on them, and they'd lost half their pots.

People in town thought her father was a little crazy, and maybe they were right. Kids at school used to call him the "mad scientist."

But if he was, then he was a wonderful, thoughtful, imaginative madman. One who loved Bonnie, fussed over her, and gave her little presents that no one else would have dreamed up in a million years: the bookmark that shut her bedroom light off when she closed the pages on it—so she wouldn't have to get out of bed—or the perfumed comb that left the subtlest, most delicious fragrance in her hair. Okay, so her father was different. And maybe that scared some folks. But for Bonnie, it was something to be proud of.

She leaned against the rail of the *Bonita II*. It wasn't that Land's End was so bad. In fact, Bonnie was sure it was one of the most beautiful spots in the world: the green hills that rolled right down to the water, the cliffs of ocher and terra-cotta with their purple shadows, the dramatic early-morning mists, the huge, rich blue skies.

Land's End even had its very own haunted house. Bonnie squinted, just able to make out the shape of the enormous villa perched on a distant cliff, its shimmering oval tower sticking up on one side like an oversized chimney. "The Lair," everyone around here called the house. It had once been the summer estate of some fabulously wealthy movie mogul who had died, along with his wife, when their private plane crashed. They'd had a son who'd survived—Bonnie remembered some of the older kids in town talking about some big Christmas party he'd given years and years ago. But no one knew what had become of him, and now the Lair was locked up tight.

Every once in a while someone claimed to have heard a terrifying roar coming from inside. It was said the place was haunted by some wild beast; dark stories circulated, which nobody really believed. Still, people generally stayed away. Once in a while someone would go up there on a dare, or a few kids would get rowdy and throw rocks and bottles from a safe distance.

"*Querida?*" Her father interrupted her thoughts, using the Portuguese word for "sweetheart." He was climbing aboard the *Bonita II,* balancing a cup of coffee in each hand. "Brought my beautiful little girl a piping-hot cup of morning wake-up." His fondness for American expressions was a funny contrast to his gentle foreign accent. "Almost burned my fingers carrying it," he went on. "Which gave me an idea for a new invention . . ."

Bonnie laughed. What would it be this time? A coffee glove? A special insulated cup? A stirring stick that automatically regulated the temperature of your beverage? "Why don't you tell me about it on our way out of here?" She took her coffee from her father and made a tiny tear in the plastic top. "The tide's going out, and we've gotta get moving if we want to clear the harbor floor," she reminded him.

"Anchors away, then," her father agreed.

Bonnie took a sip of hot coffee, and with her free hand she began untying the *Bonita II* from its mooring. Too bad they weren't taking off for somewhere far, far away . . . .

Two

The beast watched the little boat with the crazy gadgets as it pulled out of the harbor. Out across the silver-blue water it went, rolling gently with the movements of the waves and tide, out to where there was only sea and sky. Free. Oh, so free. The beast let out a low, mournful growl. What wonderfully lucky souls were working those sails?

Way, way down in the little town, the day was beginning. Even with his animal vision, the houses and roads and cars were like miniatures in a dollhouse village from here. But the beast imagined the scene as large as life.

"Have a good day. I love you," couples said to each other as they kissed good-bye.

"You're it!" a big brother called out, tagging the younger one as they roughhoused on their way to school.

"Nice day," one neighbor commented to another when they passed on the sidewalk.

They were down there in the town—people connecting with other people. Live and in person. The beast turned away from the window, dropping down on all fours and curling up on the floor. His bed stood in one corner of the room, but he barely used it anymore. He hadn't for many years. Every evening Rita, his childhood nanny, turned down the covers. And every night the beast slept on the floor. Then every morning Rita made the bed up again.

Once upon a time it had been different. Once upon a time he'd dreamed happily there in cozy warmth under a fluffy down comforter. Once upon a time he'd been as free as that little boat bobbing on the water, as much a person as the people down in the dollhouse town. Once upon a time he'd been a real boy. A human being.

The beast's strong, sinewy muscles tensed under a thick coat of golden fur. Gone. Those days were over. The days when he'd been human. It was so long ago that it almost seemed like a dream. But what he remembered as acutely as the tempting scent of prey was the night his boyhood had been taken away from him.

It had been a cold, black night. No moon. No

stars. Just a thick fog and a shrill wind whistling through bare branches. The ocean raged down below the cliffs, pounding against the rocks and throwing up angry, electric bursts of water, sounding like bombs exploding.

But inside the huge house, it was warm and bright. "Merry Christmas," a boy's voice called out. Every light burned brightly. A crackling fire roared in the fireplace in the oversized main room. The boy—his name was Peter—was throwing a holiday party at his vacation home. All the boys and girls from town were there, as well as many children from the city in which Peter lived. Maybe they weren't exactly his friends. But he'd lured them there with a lavish feast and toys and presents for everyone, a skating rink out back with music pouring onto the ice—and they could keep the skates he'd gotten for them to use.

". . . sleigh bells ring . . ." came the music from out back.

And there was a mammoth Christmas tree in front of the house, ablaze with lights and shiny ornaments. "It's the largest tree anywhere in the county," Peter told them; he'd given orders for that.

He surveyed the party, prince of all he saw. Kids were laughing and playing, dancing to a live band. Two girls came in from skating, pink-cheeked and smiling. "How do you like my party?" he asked.

"This is the best party we've ever been to," they told him.

Peter felt something close to happiness. Satisfaction, maybe. All those kids were there and having a great time because of him. He almost stopped feeling the gaping emptiness that had been inside him since his parents' accident. The servants rushed around. "We need more chocolate-marshmallow-supreme pie," he told the short, wiry one named Arno.

"Right away, Master Peter," the tuxedoed servant said.

Then Peter watched as his soft-faced, round-bodied nanny made her way through the crowd of kids toward him. He felt a tickle of annoyance. Rita had made it quite clear that she thought he was going way too far that night.

"Other young people get together and sing a few Christmas carols," she'd told him when he was planning the celebration, her sweet face unusually stern. "They drink a glass of eggnog together, maybe exchange a few inexpensive trinkets, and then go home to their families. They don't spend a king's ransom on a children's party."

"Well, I don't have a family to go home to," Peter had retorted.

Her stern expression had melted. "You have me, little Peter. Never forget that. I know I can't ever replace your mother and father, but when you were a baby, I held you when you cried. I taught you to sing. I fed you. I cared for you. I'm sorry I'm not enough, but you're not as alone as you think."

Peter frowned as Rita approached him. She'd tried to sweet-talk him out of this wonderful party—*his* party. But he was the boss. He feared she'd tell him that it was time for his guests to go on home. *Well, she can forget that,* he thought. *The party's still going strong, and I'm not ready for it to end.*

But she said something else. "Peter, there's a woman at the door."

"A woman? Who? The mother of one of my guests? Coming to take someone home from my party?"

Rita shook her head. "She wants to speak to the master of the house."

Peter felt a puff of pride. "That's me. Well, I hope she has a good reason for interrupting me in the middle of all this." He ignored Rita's frown and headed for the heavy oak door. He peered out into the night with the barest touch of curiosity.

On the front step stood an old, old woman—way older than Rita. She was the sorriest specimen of a person he'd ever seen. Peter instantly recoiled. Her thick, yellowed gray hair hung in knotted strands. Her heavily lined face was raw and chapped from the cold, and her eyes were puffy. She rubbed her leathery hands together as she cast Peter a pathetic, pleading look.

"Yes?" he asked. "I'm in the middle of hosting a huge party," he added, feeling important as he thought of all his guests.

"You must be a very fine young boy to live in a house like this and host such a grand affair," the ugly old woman said. Her voice was surprisingly fresh and strong, as if there were another woman inside this one.

Peter felt even prouder. "Well, yes, I suppose that's true."

"And it must be so warm and inviting inside," she continued. "It's so bitterly cold. My stomach is empty, and I've nowhere to sleep tonight."

So that was what this frightful old woman wanted from him. Peter's pride turned to anger. "And why are you telling *me* this?" How dare the old woman come begging at his door?

"Won't you take pity on someone less fortunate than yourself?" she asked. "I'd be so very, very grateful. You have so much. Won't you share just a very tiny, little bit?"

"I *am* sharing. My guests all have bags and bags of presents, and who do you think bought them? Now, if you'll excuse me, I have a party going on inside."

"I'd be gone by morning."

"We could perhaps put her up in the pool house," suggested Rita, who was standing a few steps behind Peter. "She won't trouble you back there. You won't even know she's there."

Peter turned, scowling. "And what will she give us?"

The old woman let out a long breath, and Peter felt a sudden blast of cold air whip in from outside. Suddenly her hand reached out to the winter-barren rosebush canes climbing the trellis-work at the entrance to the house. And then she held out a perfect, full, deep pink rose. She stretched her arm out, offering it to Peter.

"How did you do that?" Peter asked. "I didn't see that there. It's just not possible that— Well, never mind. You offer me a flower from my very own garden? You're a thief as well as a beggar."

The wind swirled viciously. "I offer you a

sweet, lovely drop of summer in the winter, a thing of perfection . . ."

The old woman looked even uglier by comparison to the rose in her hand. Peter was repulsed. "Silly woman, I have whatever I want. Can't you see that?" He gestured grandly to his house and possessions. "Now, away with you."

Rita edged forward. Peter felt her trying to squeeze by him. "I'm sorry," she said to the old woman. "His parents died a number of years ago. I'm afraid his behavior is partially my fault. I may have spoiled him to make up for suffering such a tragic loss."

"Are you calling me spoiled?" Peter said in a fury. "I don't see you or any of the other servants complaining about all the wads of money my parents left you to see me to adulthood. So don't complain about me!" he commanded.

He heard Rita's sharp intake of breath, but she said nothing at all.

"And you." He whirled back toward the old woman. "You'd best be gone. We don't allow trespassers here."

"Don't you have an ounce of humanity?" the old woman asked. And then there was a change in the way she looked. The yellowed gray hair became silvery blond. The chapped cheeks turned rosy, full of power and life. Her wrinkles faded. Peter blinked hard. He couldn't be seeing this.

"No, you don't. No humanity at all," she said, her voice stronger than ever and deepening commandingly. "You are nothing but a beast." She seemed to grow in front of his eyes. She, he— Peter could no longer say which. Straight back, strong body, and bright, angry expression. Not old but not young. The being had transformed before his own eyes.

He became dizzy with shock. He felt it in his limbs as a kind of yawning ache. The ache deepened. He glanced down at himself and let out a raw cry. He'd changed, too. His fingers had thickened, his hands had swelled. His nails had lengthened, sharpened. A thick fur had grown on them, the same dark blond as his hair. *Oh, no!* he thought. *What's happening?*

Every part of his body had begun to hurt. His arms and legs and torso. His face—he felt it twist uncontrollably. He put his hand to it. But his hand—it had become a paw, and his face had lengthened out at the mouth, and his nose was now pointy, soft, wet. His face was covered with fur, too. He felt it with the pads of his paw. His teeth felt too big and sharp in his mouth. He heard the furious rip of clothes as his mutated body burst their seams. He let out the roar of a wild animal.

"Peter! My little Peter!" Rita cried in terror.

"No!" he howled. "Oh, no, no!" His little boy's voice emerged from this alien form.

"You behaved like a beast, and now you are one," the being on his doorstep said.

"Oh, please! I'm sorry. Maybe I was hasty." Peter—the beast—began to shiver and shake. "Spend the night here. You're welcome to be my guest. Anything you wish. Only change me back. Oh, please change me back!"

"No," came the thundering reply. "But I *will* leave you with this rose you so cavalierly refused—this single, perfect rose. You are a beast now, and so you shall stay until you reach the age of twenty-one. If by then you have learned what it means to be human—to feel and to love and to have another human being love you—then you will become human once more."

"And if not . . ." The beast's words sounded more like whimpering yelps.

"Then you will remain a beast forever!" the enchantress at his door thundered.

A crashing wave echoed along the cliffs. And

the powerful being suddenly vanished into the fog.

"But how could anyone love a beast like this?" The mournful question melted into a dismal yowl. The beast was doomed forever.

Three

"Ooh, I just love a girl in boots," Gary Belsky was saying as he and his sidekicks, Pat and Mark, trailed Bonnie down the main street of Land's End.

Bonnie rolled her eyes. The solid ground under her knee-high rubber fishing boots still felt a little strange after the constant rocking of the little boat.

"Gary, give me a break. If you don't mind, I worked hard today." She could feel the result of hours of sun and salt wind on her face, and her arms were tired from pulling up and lowering lobster pots. All she wanted to do was pick up something easy to make for dinner and read a good book. Preferably one set in some faraway place. Fending off Gary Belsky was not in the plan.

"Yeah, I'll bet. All that hauling and lifting

and heavy work. A beautiful girl shouldn't have to do that."

"Oh, please, Gary. You think we should just stay home and embroider little pillow covers?" Bonnie asked lightly.

One of his friends snickered.

"Well, it's just that if you were mine, you wouldn't *have* to work so hard, is all I meant." Gary patted his tool belt in a macho gesture.

"That's right," Pat said. "Big man Gary builds big houses. Gets big paycheck. Takes care of little woman." He punched Mark in the arm, as if he'd said the funniest thing in the world. The two of them burst out laughing.

"Yo, shut up," Gary said. "Don't forget you guys are working for me these days. You want me to hire you for any more jobs, you better pipe down."

"Oops! Sorry, boss," Pat guffawed, not sounding too worried.

Bonnie crossed the street in front of the tiny town hall and headed into the grocery store. Gary and company followed. "Making the two of us something good to eat?" he persisted. "Candlelit dinner and everything?"

Bonnie gave a sharp click of her tongue. "Knuckle sandwich is about all I want to serve you."

"Mmm, I love it when you talk rough to me, honey."

She got a basket and put a package of cheese ravioli in it. "Think you could go bother someone else for a while?"

"Ah, my sweet Bonnie," Gary said. "Why do you want to break my heart?"

"Yo, boss, what's the big deal?" Mark spoke up in his slow, hazy-headed way. He let his finger trail along one of the store's shelves. "Chick's too weird, anyway. Thinks she's too good for us here in Land's End."

Bonnie ignored him. She threw some Parmesan cheese into her basket.

"Mark, the chick's name is Bonnie. We've been in school with her since first grade, so you ought to know that," Gary said. "You also ought to know that she's the most beautiful girl in town." Gary beamed at Bonnie as if she were supposed to be bowled over by his flattery.

"But Gary, Mark's right," Pat told him. "She doesn't want to stick around here, hook up with some guy who pounds nails. 'To boldly go where I haven't gone before,'" he said, quoting her yearbook page.

Bonnie felt an angry blush creeping across her cheeks. She dropped a head of lettuce in her basket.

When Pat quoted her, he made her sound like a snob. Why was it so terrible to want to have adventures, to see some of the world, to be open to new places and new people?

"Okay, so maybe she needs a little reforming," Gary said easily. "I like the challenge. Turn her into a good little woman to come home to after a long day of work."

"You wish," Bonnie said. She was getting more than a little annoyed. "Isn't there a rule that you can't come in here if you're not going to shop?"

"Hey, they love me in here," Gary replied bigheadedly. "They're happy to have me around. You should be, too."

"You just want her because she's the only girl in town you can't have," Pat observed.

Bonnie reached up on tiptoe to get a jar of olives from the top shelf.

Gary plucked it off for her and put it in her hand, letting his fingers brush hers. "Oh, but I can have her. I will have her."

Bonnie brought her groceries over to the checkout counter, relieved when Gary finally moved toward the door. "Don't hold your breath," she called after him.

*   *   *

One more deep pink petal had fallen by the base of the antique crystal vase. The beast tried clumsily to pick it up with both his paws, but it was too small and too delicate for him to grasp. He wound up crushing it and, snarling, he let it drop to the floor. The rose looked as full and beautiful and fresh as it had all those years ago, when the ugly old woman had plucked it from the bare winter branch. But the petals were starting to fall more frequently as the beast's twenty-first birthday grew ever nearer. A few more months. That was all he had left.

He turned from the pedestal on which the vase sat and stalked across the Persian carpet, shredded in many spots by his sharp claws. He reached the far wall of the main room and then headed right back to where he'd been, pacing like the caged animal he truly was in this luxury prison.

"Café l'Illusion," he spoke aloud. The room and everything in it seemed to waver and bend and blur. The furniture melted into shapeless blobs and then evaporated altogether. The walls broke apart.

And when his surroundings came into focus again, the beast was standing in a sunny cobble-stoned plaza in the south of France. Bright light washed the fountain in the center of the square, accompanied by the sound of rushing water. The café, with its outdoor seating, was off to one side. The interior smelled ever so faintly of tobacco smoke.

"Mrrr." The beast let out a satisfied purr as he strode over to one of the small, round café tables and took a seat. Well, not just any seat. In the middle of the table he chose was the deep pink rose in a simple clay vase. A man sat reading a newspaper at the table next to his. Two girls strolled around the fountain, their arms linked. An older lady walked a tiny white dog. No one stared at the beast. The man with the newspaper even nodded. "*Bonjour,*" he said.

"*Bonjour,*" replied the beast.

A waiter in a white jacket appeared from inside the café, an empty tray in his hand. Actually, it was one of the beasts' servants, Arno, dressed up as a French waiter. But he played his part perfectly, never giving any sign that the beast was anything but another of the anonymous patrons of the café.

"*Monsieur?*" he asked.

"*Un grand créme,*" the beast said, ordering a large coffee with cream.

"*Trés bien, monsieur.*" Arno headed back to the café.

The beast gave a low growl. It was very nice having coffee in a little French café. No mistake about it. But it was all smoke and mirrors. Or rather, virtual reality, and every last bit of the very latest technology that the vast wealth his parents had left him could buy.

He had the world at his fingertips. But it was a world he could never actually be part of. He would never travel to a real café in a real French town. Never nod back at the man sitting next to him or smile at those two pretty girls, one of whom was now laughing in the most carefree manner.

"*Heh-heh! Ah, c'est fantastique!*" he heard her say to her friend as a shimmery peal of laughter floated on the air. If there had been real people in this sunny square, they would have been shrieking with fear, running as fast as they could away from the beast.

And all the money in the world couldn't buy a solution. He'd tried. Oh, how he'd tried. He'd been from doctor to doctor. From miracle cure to miracle cure. He'd been poked and prodded and medicated. He'd tried strange teas and bizarre healing rituals.

He growled in disgust as he remembered the foul-tasting brew of rotten twigs and leaves he'd drunk for months and months with no results. Then he'd turned to psychologists and biologists and neurologists. Damn all of them.

As he'd gotten older, he'd arranged for a string of women guests. Real women. Sure, there were virtual women, too. Fantasies that gave the beast whatever he wanted . . . except true human companionship. But to each of the real women he'd promised all his riches if only they could fall in love with him. But not a single one had been able to do it. Not for real. So he'd sent them all away with nothing.

And he'd finally stopped trying to find a solution. He'd barricaded himself inside this place, bringing the world to him with every book he could read, every movie he could watch, and every trick a computer could possibly perform.

But no computer program could make him human. No computer would allow him to be part of the world again. And his time was running out. There was only one thing that would work.

To feel, to love, and to have another human being love you. The powerful sorcerer's words haunted him. For no one would ever love a savage beast.

The beast could see Arno bustling about inside the café. He saw a flash of Arno's white apron, heard the clatter of cups on saucers. Arno and the other servants stayed on because the beast's overly generous parents had provided for the hired help in their will. And they had only to stick it out until the beast's next birthday, when the will would set them free. Then they'd be gone. And the beast would be twenty-one. Twenty-one and legal. All alone and a monster forever.

He bared his double row of sharp teeth and snarled. Nobody paid attention. The man next to him casually flipped the page of his newspaper.

Well, there was always Rita. She, of all the servants, wouldn't leave when the beast turned twenty-one, would she? Yes, she would. Of course she would. She wasn't going to spend the rest of her life imprisoned with an animal.

Arno reappeared with a cup as big as a bowl and set it on the table. It looked like coffee. It even smelled like coffee. But what beast drinks coffee?

He lowered his face into the bowl of milk and slurped.

Four

"They're going to love me at the boat show," Bonnie's father said optimistically. "Or at least love my inventions." The bed of their beat-up truck was loaded with his crazy contraptions: the fishing rod that responded to the pressure of a bite and automatically reeled in the catch; the "salmon factory" that boned, peeled, and smoked the salmon all at once; the nautical windmill that powered a motorboat without gas.

Bonnie helped her father pull a waterproof tarp over his mechanical babies to protect them from the heavy rain that slashed her face. "I hope so, Dad," she responded, raising her voice above the gale of the summer storm.

"Oh, *querida*, they're going to discover me, and our ship will come in. We're going to be on easy street. And every street—everywhere you've ever wanted to be. That's the first thing I'll make sure of. I promise you, Bonnie. I'm going to take you all around the world, and we won't come back until you've seen everything."

Bonnie felt a rush of love for her father. But his dreams of success and wealth and around-the-world voyages—well, they were just dreams. Because no one looked at Dad and saw a genius. They looked at him and saw a kook, a guy who was off-the-wall.

Bonnie pushed a few soaking-wet strands of hair off her face. She and her father were two peas in a pod, weren't they? Dreaming their dreams that would lead to nowhere. She came around to the other side of the truck, sloshing through mud and puddles that she could barely see in the dim gray light of the afternoon downpour. She gave her father a big hug. "Good luck, Daddy."

"You bet," her father answered. "Take care of yourself until I get back. You know where to reach me if you need me." He smiled and tousled her rain-drenched hair.

A flash of lightning split the sky, followed by the crack of thunder. "You take care of yourself, too," Bonnie said. "Drive carefully, okay? It's such an awful day to be out on the road."

"Don't you worry your pretty head," her father said. "I'm just going to drive on up the coast a little ways and then head over to the superhighway at Tacumeh Grove. The driving'll be easier once I'm on the big road."

"Except that the highway turnoff is at Oceanview, not Tacumeh Grove," Bonnie said. She felt a tingle of nervous foreboding. Her father was a whiz at navigation on the boat, but back on solid ground he could be so spaced out. And the truck wasn't exactly new or trouble-free, either. "Oceanview, okay? Are you going to remember that?"

"Oceanview. Yeah, of course," her father said, kissing the top of her wet head. "Now run inside and dry off. Make yourself some hot chocolate. Relax. Read one of those books you just got out of the library. I'll be fine. And I'll miss you, *querida*."

"I'll miss you, too, Daddy. Good luck. See you in a couple of days."

Outside the wolves snarled and barked ferociously in the vicious song of a pack on the heels of a warm, bloody meal. The beast instinctively bared his teeth. His fur stood up and his ears went back flat against his head, even though the wolves couldn't possibly enter his clifftop sanctuary.

But some creature down there wasn't as lucky. A deer? A rabbit? The beast himself grew hungry at the image of fresh, juicy prey. A trickle of saliva leaked from the corner of his mouth.

But then he picked up a sound that stopped his hunger cold. "Help me!"

It was the terrified cry of a human being. The beast listened harder. Yes, there it was again. "They're going to kill me! Someone, help me!" A man's voice. A man screaming for his life. Screaming and running and panting, all at the same time—the beast could hear it. And the sounds of the wolves closing in on their meal. Deep, deep inside of him, in a place he rarely noticed any longer, the beast felt the remotest flicker of fear for the man.

But it was gone almost before it had started. What fool was out walking in the woods in the middle of a storm as the night approached fast? And why had he come so close to the beast's private refuge? The beast growled, low and soft. This place was his. It wasn't an attraction for curiosity seekers or those boys from town who tossed sticks and stones at his windows.

The beast's growl grew louder. Was it one of

those boys who was fleeing from the wolves? He'd watched them from his window the last time they'd dared to come up here. They had been three boys in ripped jeans, clutching feeble weapons—branches and bottles and rocks.

"Come out, come out, wherever you are!" one of them had taunted, waving around a broken cola bottle.

They'd flexed their muscles, but the beast had simply snorted as he watched them, unseen in the shadow of his window. *Let them come,* he'd thought. He could easily rip them limb from limb with his teeth and claws.

The adrenaline of a fight had pumped through his powerful, grotesque body. He could have silenced them almost as easily as a trio of barnyard chickens. His mouth had begun to water.

"Let's see if you're real," the tallest boy had yelled.

"I'll show you how real I am," the beast had growled, his words escalating to a roar. He'd bounded toward his door, his teeth ready to sink into their smooth, hairless shoulders, their scrawny arms and legs—arms and legs like the ones he'd had before he'd become a beast.

He'd stopped.

Those boys were what the beast once had

been. What he might have been, if only that enchantress in disguise hadn't come to his door all those years ago. He could have been one of them. He *would* have been. And that alone had stopped him from punishing them when they'd come to his gate to torment him.

But the beast was not about to save one of those boys, either. Now the cries for help drew nearer. "Please! By God, please!"

No. Whoever was out there had brought his fate upon himself by coming up here in the first place. The snarling of the wolves grew louder, too, the cries of terror more desperate. The chase was close enough for the beast to hear the twigs snapping.

And then there came a pounding on the beast's door. "Help! Please, help! Oh, no! I don't want to die!" rasped the wolves' victim.

The beast held his ground, his tense muscles not moving. If one of those juicy, meaty young men was stripped to the bones by that wolf pack, the other boys would never darken the beast's door again. Never taunt him with bottles and stones and thoughts of what he might have been. Serve them right for coming where they didn't belong. Didn't they know how lucky they were to have better things to do than to haunt this house?

"Have pity! Someone!"

The beast could feel the vibrations through his paws as the desperate victim tried to beat down the door. And then he heard a different set of footsteps inside the house. The beast recognized Rita's sturdy footfall as she broke into a run down the stairs and toward the door.

The beast sprang. In a few graceful bounds, he was out of his room and had caught Rita on the bottom step. Leaping in front of her on all fours, he blocked her way.

She stifled a cry of fear at his sudden material-ization. She was well practiced at holding back her reactions after all these years.

"Don't do a thing, do you hear me?" the beast ordered.

Rita's face had aged so since the long-ago night of the ill-fated Christmas party. When she frowned, the lines were etched even more deeply into her soft, round face. "Someone's in trouble out there," she said, her voice as stormy as the evening. "I'm going to open the door."

"This is my house!" the beast roared. "You will obey my orders."

Rita pushed him out of her way as if he were an overgrown, misbehaved pet. He sprang in front of her again, and this time his growl brought a small gasp of fear to her lips. "Don't tell me you've forgotten another time you answered the door in this house. One Christmas night. I don't have to remind you, do I? This time you'll keep that door shut."

"I beg you, open up! Someone, anyone! No! Please! They're here. I can't escape!" The horror in his voice mingled with the wolves' predatory cries.

"Listen to him, will you?" Rita said commandingly. She swallowed her fleeting fear—the beast no longer smelled it on her. "That's a man out there. A human being. Oh, perhaps it's my fault that you don't remember what it's like to be a human being anymore!"

The beast just snarled.

"Isn't there any human left in you, Peter?"

His true name was like a slap. The beast snapped his pointy muzzle shut.

"Help! Help!" came the anguished cries.

"That person out there—his life is in your hands," Rita said. She looked straight into the beast's eyes. None of the other servants ever dared do that. "That might be someone's father out there, or someone's son."

He was aware of that feeling again. The one so very deep inside. And he felt a kind of hunger in that place. A longing, a lack. And he remembered the dreadful night they'd come and told him about his parents. Rita and Arno and a man from the police force down in the town. *Someone's parent. Someone's son.*

Rita was moving toward the door. She didn't look back at the beast as she opened it. She pulled in a shaking, sopping, disheveled man. Not one of those young ones. A man in his middle years, with terror on his face.

The beast leaped toward the door and let out a resounding roar to keep the wolves at bay. He could see their glittery eyes through the pouring rain, but their snarls and cries began to die down. He threw his weight against the inside of the door and it crashed closed.

He turned to look at the man he'd saved. But now the terror on the man's face was heightened by shock. He stared at the beast, paralyzed by the sight. And the beast could see that the man was deathly afraid—afraid he might have been better off outside with the wolves.

There was an insistent knocking at the door.

"Coming," Bonnie yelled as she put her book down unwillingly. She pulled herself up out of the old, comfortable armchair in which she'd been curled up reading. "Who is it?" she added, mildly annoyed. It was too late in the evening for visitors.

Her father had been gone only a day, and she didn't expect him home so soon. But maybe he'd come home earlier than he'd planned. Had the real world disappointed him again? Had he and his inventions been giggled out of the boat show? She imagined him knocking with one hand while he fumbled for his keys with the other, too distraught and angry to find what he was looking for.

Bonnie crossed the braided rug and the wide-planked wooden floor of their little house. She had been far off in early twentieth-century Spain, getting lost in Ernest Hemingway's tales of brave bullfighters and wild feasts of food and drink. She'd been imagining herself as a Spanish senorita with flowers in her hair, dancing in some crowded little bar with a handsome senor.

Now she grudgingly opened her front door just wide enough to see who was out there. "Well, hey, Bonnie." Gary Belsky looked back at her, smiling his maddeningly full-of-himself smile. Definitely not the guy she'd just been daydreaming about. Or ever would daydream about. She wished she'd left the door closed.

"Yeah?" she asked warily, not opening the door any farther. She didn't want Gary to get the idea that he was welcome here. He'd probably come to apologize for Pat and Mark's moronic behavior in the grocery store the other day. Well, she thought, let him say his piece as fast as possible and then leave her to get back to her book.

But Gary had no apology in mind. "Hey, Bon," he said, as if they were the closest of friends. "What are you up to this potentially romantic evening?"

Bonnie couldn't believe the nerve of him. Hadn't she made it clear that she wasn't interested? "I'm reading," she said flatly. "At least I was until you interrupted me."

Gary pushed the door open. "How lonely," he said, leaning close to her. "Wanna do something about it?"

Bonnie pulled away instantly. "Actually, it's not lonely at all," she retorted. "In fact, I was just in a huge bullring with thousands of screaming fans, a handsome matador, and a fierce, angry bull."

Gary knit his eyebrows as if Bonnie were crazy. "You were where? With a handsome who? I thought you said you were reading."

"Well, I wasn't *really* in a bullring," Bonnie

said. "I meant that's what I was in the middle of reading about." Boy, was this guy a loser.

Gary tried to take a step inside, but Bonnie blocked his way. It brought them face to face. "And this Matty guy—was he as handsome as I am?"

"Matador," Bonnie said with annoyance. "He's the one who kills the bull." At that moment she wished she were the *matador* and Gary were the bull. A long steel sword with a sharp point would be helpful in getting rid of this turkey.

Gary laughed condescendingly. "Come on down to the planet Earth with the rest of us, Bonnie. It's Friday night. Forget your little bookworm fantasies. People are out there having fun."

Bonnie felt a stab of loneliness. She *did* wish she were out having a romantic evening with a wonderful guy, instead of just reading about having fun. Maybe they'd walk on the beach and look at the stars, or watch a good movie, or share a delicious dinner. But Gary wasn't that guy. Far from it.

"You've got a real, live, red-blooded *American* guy at your door," Gary prompted.

"Who was just about to leave," Bonnie said flatly.

Gary's expression grew dark. "I don't know,

Bonnie. Maybe I should be paying more attention to what Pat and Mark say about you. You're getting a reputation with some people for being pretty unfriendly. You wouldn't want me to start believing that, would you?"

Bonnie pushed the door closed even as she spoke. "Believe what you want. Just as long as you quit bugging me, okay?"

Gary's angry reply was muffled by the door. "You know, Bonnie, one day you'll be sorry you weren't nicer to me. One day you'll need me, and we'll see who calls the shots then."

Bonnie went back to her book and her cozy armchair. "Fat chance," she said out loud.

Five

"Wh-what do you plan to do with me?" the man asked fearfully. His repulsion as he gazed at the beast was palpable.

The beast had carefully dressed himself to present a casual, civilized picture—jeans that were tailored for his animal form, a pair of fine leather slippers on his rear paws, even a book facedown on the little table next to him. Not that the beast's clumsy paws could turn the pages without the aid of a tool he'd had specially designed for him. But the man didn't have to know about that. So here the beast sat, as human, he hoped, as an inhuman creature could manage to be.

But the beast knew the trembling man wasn't fooled. The beast could smell his terror. And his eyes were bright with something even worse for the beast to see than fear. It was the gleam of repulsion and disbelief, the inability to accept that the gruesome, unnatural creature before him was real.

"I-I'm indebted to you for saving my life," the man whispered hoarsely, barely able to get a shaky sentence out. "But surely you don't intend to keep me here, do you?" He stared at the beast the way one might stare at a fatal car crash—not wanting to see the grim spectacle, but unable to tear one's eyes away, either.

The beast imagined himself as the man saw him—huge, hairy paws bursting from the sleeves of his shirt, pointy ears, and beady eyes. A form built for the chase, and razor-sharp teeth made for the kill. A creature of the wild squeezed into an armchair in a pathetic imitation of what he was not. Only the instinctual control of a beast that must silently stalk its prey kept him from letting loose a piteous yowl.

"You've seen my horrible face," the beast growled. The man's every frightened gesture confirmed just how awful the beast was to behold. "Do you think I'll let you tell the world what kind of freak I am? Tell the people in your town that a monster lives in their backyard? How long do you think they would leave me alone?"

"Oh, please, I won't tell a soul," the man said.

"My lips are sealed. It would be as if I'd never been here. I swear it. Cross my fingers. You have my word."

The beast gave a low, throaty growl. "Your word. And if you go back on it? Don't you think the people outside my walls would tear me to bits if they knew I existed? It's your word against my life—as repulsive a life as you may think it is."

"Please, sir. I don't think that. I—I don't think anything at all, do you hear me? I haven't even seen you, if anyone asks. I've never been inside your walls. It wasn't my fault that I got lost on the road or that my truck broke down. All I was doing was looking for help when those wolves caught my scent. They chased me here. I wound up at your door without any choice. So I beg you not to keep me locked up." His eyes automatically traveled upward toward the oval tower where the beast had ordered him held under lock and key.

"Yes, the sky room," the beast said. "Fine view, every luxury money can buy. Lots of important people stayed in that room in the days when— Well, forget about that." He gave a sudden roar.

The man quivered at the sound. "It's a beautiful room," he finally managed. "And I'm sure the people who stayed there were far more important than I am. But I look out all those windows and all I can see is the ocean where my boat should be, and the valley where my little house is and—oh, if you have a shred of feeling in you—where my daughter is waiting for me. My beautiful daughter . . ."

"Your daughter?" So Rita had been right. The man was a father after all. The beast had a distant, foggy image of his own father holding tight to his hand as he taught his little son to jump the waves at the ocean's edge.

"Here it comes! One, two . . . over! Wow, that's cold water!" His father's voice echoed far away and long ago.

Had that ever really happened? Had the beast ever been that carefree little boy? The image was so weak, the beast couldn't hold it for long. It eluded him like a tender, juicy rabbit, escaping behind the nearest bush in a rush of adrenaline-fueled fear. All that was left for the beast was an empty hunger.

"Tell me about your daughter," he commanded.

"She's the most special girl in the world," the man said. "Smart and energetic, and as pretty to look at as—"

"As a rose in bloom?" the beast asked with a glance at the fateful pink rose in its vase on its pedestal. Thank goodness another velvety petal hadn't fallen from the flower. But it was only a matter of time before it would.

The man nodded. "Even prettier. And she's all I've got in this world. Oh, if you don't let me return to her—"

"Silence!" the beast roared. "Some of us have no one at all. Now I want to hear more about this girl who is lovelier than a rose. I want to know everything about her." How often he'd stared down at the little town in the valley and wondered about the people who lived there.

"Well, my daughter celebrated her eighteenth birthday not long ago—a few weeks before she graduated from high school," the man said. The beast nodded for him to continue, and the man obeyed. "She and her friend Doris went out sailing and had a picnic on one of the little islands you can see from up here."

The beast settled back into his chair as he did when he watched a good movie on his state-of-the-art TV. "And now?" he coaxed the man to continue.

"Now she's helping on my lobster boat."

The beast could sense the fear going out of the

man as he slipped into thoughts of his precious daughter.

"She's working with me and dreaming about something better, I'm afraid," the man said with a soft, sad laugh.

The beast inclined his huge head. He knew about dreams.

"She loves to read." The man gestured at the beast's open book. "She's gone through just about everything in the Land's End library. She swims like a mermaid. And she loves to dance."

"With the boys in the town?" the beast asked.

"Sometimes. They have lots of dances and parties at her school."

The beast tried to picture himself spinning through a noisy, crowded room with a girl. A pretty girl like this man's daughter. "What does she look like?" he wanted to know.

"Tall and graceful with long, light brown hair and smooth, pale skin. Big blue eyes. A beautiful smile."

The beast added this information to his fantasy dance. His limbs grew restless as his mind took him twirling in perfect rhythm with his graceful, imaginary partner. The music was slow and dreamy. The lights were soft and low. Her hair was silky and smelled of wild grasses. The beast purred quietly in the back of his throat.

"So you'll let me return to her?" The man's voice interrupted the beast's rapture.

The beast let out a snarl. "Who told you that?"

The man gave a frightened start. "I thought . . . I'd hoped that perhaps you were beginning to see. . . ." His eyes grew wet. "I love my daughter so much. Can't you understand that?"

The beast's glance went to the rose again. "What does a beast know about love?" he asked.

"Then you won't let me go?" the man cried. "You're going to keep me locked up in here? You might as well have left me to the wolves. You truly are a beast!"

The beast sprang out of his chair with an angry hiss. "And so I am. But I'm a beast who saved your life. So humor me. Humor a lonely beast for a few days with your stories and your company. You owe me that much."

"And then will you let me go?"

The fight went out of the beast. He was thirsty. So thirsty for the little details of ordinary life that this man had to offer. "Then we'll see."

It had been too long. Bonnie pedaled her bike along the sandy shoulder of Heron Pond Road, away from the new police station. Ralph Belsky, the chief of police and Gary's uncle, insisted that it was too soon even to worry, let alone to consider searching for her father.

"An adult person is not considered missing until there has been no sign of said person for at least one month," Chief Belsky had quoted from some invisible book of rules. "Or in the case of someone like your father—who's maybe a little, shall we say, flaky—perhaps more like two months would be in order." He'd chuckled as if this were some kind of joke. "The mad scientist might have decided to take off in hot pursuit of some secret project."

Bonnie pedaled hard and angrily as the conversation replayed in her mind. "My father is *not* a mad scientist, and he would *never* just disappear without telling me," she'd yelled at the police chief.

"Hey, hey, pretty little lady." He'd put his hands up in front of him. "Just trying to keep things light. You *did* say your father had taken some of his wacky inventions over to the boat show in Salina Marshes, didn't you? And you did say you weren't sure exactly how long he was going to stay, yes?"

"I said he wasn't sure whether he was going to

stay one day or two," Bonnie had said, her voice getting louder. "It's been three, and we were supposed to work today."

"So maybe he finally got a bite on one of those crazy toys of his," Chief Belsky had said. "You know? Maybe there's someone out there who doesn't mind getting stuck in the middle of the ocean when the wind gives out on that windmill number he cooked up. Could be that some ecology freak paid your father good money for that thing. Suppose that's the case, okay? So Tony Olivieree's finally sold one of his nutty inventions, and he decides to celebrate, take a day off. He's sure as sugar been waiting for that sale to happen, hasn't he, little lady?"

Bonnie shook with anger just remembering the police chief's words. She had to steady herself on her bicycle. She hadn't bothered to tell him that the wind-powered boat had an emergency motor, or that her name was decidedly not "little lady," or that she thought he purposely mangled the pronunciation of *Oliviera* just to show how foreign it was.

"My father intended to work today, and he doesn't miss a day out on the boat unless there's a major storm blowing," she'd told Chief Belsky. "Maybe you don't take your job as seriously as he does."

Chief Belsky's puffy, ruddy face had grown even redder. "Now listen here, young lady. It's a damn good thing that you're a special friend of my nephew, or I'd throw you right out of this station for talking to me that way."

Eventually the police chief had made a few phone calls, put out a few bulletins to make sure there hadn't been any accidents between Land's End and Salina Marshes. "But I'm only doing it for Gary," he'd said.

Bonnie swerved to avoid a hazardous patch of sand in the road. Those Belskys were beasts. She clicked the gearshift into low as she worked her way up a steep hill. Riding over the top, she saw the ocean winking in the sunlight. It was a perfect early-summer day, the wild dune roses sweet in the air, a mild breeze carrying the warmth of the lazy days to come, the sound of waves lapping at the shore. But the beautiful weather only made Bonnie more anxious. How could everything seem so normal when she was sure something was so wrong?

"Oh, Dad," she said out loud. Why couldn't Chief Belsky find out anything? Bonnie coasted down the other side of the hill, picking up too much speed but not bothering to put the brakes on. And was Gary Belsky really going around talking as though they were actually a couple?

It sure would have been nice to have someone special at a time like this. To assure her everything was going to be all right. To hold her and help her figure out some kind of plan, some way to bring her father back.

And, of course, she dreamed about someone to share the sweeter moments with, too. But Gary Belsky wouldn't be the one if he were the last man on earth. The nerve of him, letting his uncle think they were together. His uncle and who else in Land's End? Bonnie would have been furious if she hadn't been so consumed by worry about her father.

"Come back in a few days if you haven't heard anything from your father by then," Gary's uncle had said.

But she couldn't wait that long. There wasn't any reason to wait. If her father had sold one of his inventions, he would have come home to celebrate with her. If he'd decided to stay away an extra day, he would have called. She knew there was something very wrong. Was her father lying hurt and helpless on some out-of-the-way road where he'd taken a wrong turn? She remembered how he'd almost gotten lost before he'd even gotten into his truck, how she'd had to remind him that the highway interchange was at Oceanview instead of Tacumeh Grove.

Well, she couldn't just sit around and do nothing until Chief Belsky got good and ready to help her. She was going to have to go out and look for her father herself.

Six

The beast smacked his lips in anticipation as the man—Antonio—stepped into the living room. He watched Tony's mouth open in recognition and shock—and, yes, pleasure.

The beast had gotten to know quite a lot about his visitor and his visitor's life. He knew what Tony's days were like, from the moment Tony woke up in his small but comfortable redwood house, to his coffee-and-doughnut breakfast at the place called the Foghorn, to his day at sea on the *Bonita II*, and on until he said good night to his beautiful daughter Bonnie and went to bed.

Of Bonnie, the beast had truly hunted for every detail. The tiny birthmark on her shoulder, her favorite authors, her favorite color, her favorite meal. In his mind he'd danced with Bonnie many times since that first time, keeping her away from all those boys with sticks and stones and bottles who didn't deserve her.

And he knew about Tony's hometown in Portugal. With green hills rolling down to the ocean, it mirrored the very landscape here. But Tony hadn't seen that town in so long. The beast had listened to his dreams of walking the cozily narrow streets again, visiting the whitewashed houses and sunny little main square up on a hilltop. He even knew about the little coffee bar Tony remembered his father and grandfather going to when he was a small boy.

The beast knew about it and, as a surprise, had programmed his dream machine to recreate it. What an expression on Tony's face as he looked around! The beast purred. Oh, it was so nice to have a guest in the house.

"What do you think?" he finally asked as Tony stared at the row upon row of colored bottles on the shelves behind the virtual bar. The big brass coffee machine hissed away as Arno, sporting a black beret, made inky black coffee and steamed up milk noisily in a metal pitcher. The beast let out an impatient roar.

Silent with what seemed to be shock, Tony ran his hand along the heavy wooden bar. At one end sat the pink rose in a ceramic vase. He scanned the rows of darkly gleaming bottles, labeled in his native Portuguese. Tony went closer to one wall to inspect the bold, vaguely Arabic-looking patterns on the colorful, highly glazed ceramic tiles.

"The Bar Passatempo. I'll be a monkey's uncle." He smiled, his face filled with nostalgia, and the beast could feel the corners of his own mouth pulling up.

But then Tony's smile slipped away. He sank down at one of the small tables in the dark, narrow room. "What do I think of it?" he asked. "I think it's wonderful, but I'd prefer to go home to my daughter and my life," he said softly.

The beast couldn't hold back a fierce howl. "Look what I did for you, you ungrateful man! I brought your precious Bar Passatempo all the way from across the ocean, and you don't even thank me. After all our talks, after all you've told me about your life, I thought we might even be friends." He gave a snort. "But a man like you would never be friends with a beast like me."

Tony took the coffee that Arno brought him. "Don't feel so sorry for yourself," he said wearily. "How could I be your friend when you hold me here against my will? When you order me to talk and insist that it's friendship. When you command me to feel that an illusion of a memory is better than real life and real love."

The beast whimpered like a tame pet. "Oh, why can't you forget about your unimportant life for a few days?"

"And then a few days more and a few days more," Tony said. "You don't intend to let me go. And you're trying to buy my friendship. But it won't work. Not even this global amusement park, as amazing as it is, could be enough to make me forget about my family and my home." He took a sip of the coffee. "Ahhh. You even got the recipe right. Very impressive. A beast, but a cultured one. You know, I don't even think you intend to hurt me, do you? Still, there's a giant lock on the door to my fancy room, and I'm your prisoner while my daughter is probably sick with worry." He looked down into his coffee cup. "Which makes you nothing but a hateful animal."

"A hateful animal? I give you the best gift I can think of, and I'm a hateful animal?" Even Arno jumped at the beast's angry roar. "So you don't like it. Okay." He took a heavy paw and knocked over rows of bottles as easily as a row of dominoes. The smell of alcohol followed the crash of glass, and puddles spread out on the floor.

He'd spared nothing in this gift for his guest. But all Tony wanted was his insignificant life in his insignificant town. The beast bared his teeth and bit into whatever was nearest—furniture, glasses, the signs behind the bar. He tugged at the carefully concealed wires that made these illusions possible.

He roared, and the sound shook the wooden floor of the virtual bar. He attacked the lifeless objects around him as if they were the enemy, converting wild energy into damage. He gnashed his teeth, the warm, salty taste of his own blood running into his mouth as the Bar Passatempo disappeared. And then, without pause, he ripped the stuffing out of his own furniture, destroying his cozy reading chair, knocking over lamps. . . .

He sensed movement out of the corner of his eye. Suddenly he found himself springing in front of the door to the big room as Tony and Arno tried to run for cover. He growled low and dangerously. Crouching in front of them, he got set to lunge.

"What on earth is going on in here?" Rita's voice worked its way through his animal rage. She stepped into his peripheral vision, hand on one doughy hip. "What could you possibly be thinking? Or don't you think at all anymore?"

The racing of blood through the beast's veins began to slow. His muscles started to give up their tension. "Look at what you've done!" Rita exclaimed. "Look at *you!*"

The two men cautiously moved out of their corner. They were staring at him, too. And what was it they saw? The beast didn't have to look in a mirror. He knew his eyes were wild and his clothes were ripped. Blood smeared the floor amid sharp chips of glass and splintered furniture. Drool worked its way out of his mouth. Feathers and upholstery stuffing clung to his fur as if he had just killed a whole barnyard of fowl. The beast wanted to vanish into nothing, like the Bar Passatempo.

The man Tony was right. The beast was nothing more than a hateful animal. And just to taunt him with that, there on the floor in the middle of all the damage lay the one perfect pink rose. Its vase was shattered, and one more petal had worked its way off the bloom.

Tacumeh Grove. The old road crept cracked and untended through a dark, muddy stretch of woods. The trees closed low overhead. Just about no one came this way anymore, since the new highway had been built. But Bonnie was ready to bet dollars to doughnuts, as her father might have said, that he'd been driving their old truck here through that storm.

"Oh, Dad," she whispered to the trees.

Her legs ached from cycling all the way from Land's End. The sweat she'd worked up earlier in the ride made her feel wet and chilly now that the sun was sinking lower. Night was only a few hours away. Bonnie kept her eyes focused for any clue—a stray tire track, a road her father might have turned on to. But there was nothing, and she was smack in the middle of nowhere.

"Just a little farther," she told herself, but she couldn't hold back a shiver of fear. If she made it to Portville, Doris had a friend there whom she could call for a place to stay. But Portville was almost as far ahead as Land's End was back the way she'd come. *Should I give up?* Bonnie wondered. *Turn around and go home?* But what was the point of returning home, where she'd be too panicked to do anything but pace the house like a trapped animal?

Up ahead, an arc-shaped spur of road split off from the main straightaway, leading to an abandoned-looking rest area, and then curved back to the main road again. Bonnie's muscles felt heavy from exertion. Maybe if she pulled over for a few moments, she'd have the energy to keep pushing on. She needed to rest her legs, maybe have one of the sandwiches she'd packed in her knapsack. She was too worried to have an appetite, but her stomach was churning. She knew she ought to eat something.

She steered into the rest area, which consisted of a brick building with its windows boarded up and a few pitted picnic tables and benches. *A good spot for a hideout, or a horror story,* she thought. It gave her the creeps. She got off her bike and walked it over to one of the tables. She'd just bolt down a sandwich, let her legs rest for a moment, and get going again. She didn't want to stay here any longer than that. She looked around suspiciously, half expecting someone unsavory to be lurking around.

She imagined the newspaper headlines: *Land's End Girl Dies in Gruesome Ritual.* Had something like that happened to her father? She was alert for breaking twigs and fleeting movements. What if someone was right behind the brick building, over by the—

By their brown truck, half concealed by the rusty old Dumpster at the far end of the rest-stop parking lot!

"I knew it!" Bonnie exclaimed, letting her bicycle

crash to the ground as she ran over to the truck as fast as she could push her tired legs. Her throat tightened with fear at what she might find.

As she drew near she could see the bulk of her father's inventions under the tarp in the back of the truck. Up front, the cab appeared empty. She pulled open the driver's-side door. Yes, it was empty. Bonnie wasn't sure whether to feel more or less worried. On the passenger's seat was a pair of orange work gloves, covered with grease, as if her father had been fiddling with a bum engine. Nothing else. No other clue about where he might be or could have gone.

Bonnie climbed out of the truck and made a circle around it. Dad had gotten lost. The truck had given out. He would have had to go for help. But where? Bonnie looked around. The deserted road cut through thick forest. Okay, maybe once in a while someone did drive by. But on the day her father had left? In that raging storm? He would have been on his own that evening.

Bonnie wasn't sure what to do. "Dad, where are you?" she whispered, her voice shaky with frustration and fear. She looked over at the mountains and at the little patch of sky that was visible ahead, above the road. The sky was darkening. She looked up. And suddenly she was gripped with a deep, cold terror. There, high up on the summit of the mountain at the base of which she stood, a huge house was silhouetted against the sky. She knew that house. She recognized its shape, though she was used to seeing it from a different point of view. But there was the oval turret at one side of the house, poking up like a giant straw from the main building. She'd seen it so many times from the beach down the coast.

"The Lair!"

Bonnie's breath came fast and shallow. Her pulse raced out of control. The Lair! And it was the only building as far as the eye could see. Had her father gone there looking for help? Didn't he know the stories people told about it? *Oh, Dad.* Bonnie wept silently. Was he inside that infamous place?

There was only one way to find out.

Bonnie pounded at the Lair's heavy door. Her heart beat just as hard. "Daddy!" she called at the top of her lungs. "Daddy, are you inside there?"

It was probably a hopeless quest. The latticework archway outside the entrance to the house was falling apart. Dead vines clung to it, and the paint was peeling. The grass on the lawn had grown long and wild, and the flower beds were nothing but weeds and mud. Clearly the place was abandoned. No one had lived here for years. Who could believe the myths and stories about the Lair? And here was Bonnie, all alone, as the sky grew dusky purple and the air took on a chill. And her father? Who knew where he might be?

Bonnie sucked in a startled breath as the door was pulled open. Suddenly she found herself staring at a sight that was so terrifying, she couldn't even get out a scream.

The thing filled the doorway. This . . . creature . . . seemed to be part animal, part man. The face was like a nightmare morph of a grizzly bear and a wolf and a hyena. The huge, hairy body was erect like a human but infinitely more frightening. The tailored clothes were bizarrely out of place on the animal form. Her blood went cold. What monster was this?

And then he opened up his snout, revealing double rows of blade-sharp teeth, and spoke her name. He spoke! "You're Bonnie, aren't you?" he said.

Bonnie's terror turned to shock and amazement. And then back to terror again as her father's voice broke her startled silence. "Bonnie?

Bonnie, run!" he called from somewhere inside the house.

"Daddy! Oh, Daddy, are you all right?"

"Forget about me and get out of here as fast as you can!" her father yelled. "Hurry! Go! Before it's too late."

But the talking creature—the monster who knew her name—was already taking hold of her sleeve with his teeth and forcing her inside. The heavy door slammed shut. There was no escape. The animal pulled her into the next room. And there stood her father, surrounded by the smashed and broken remains of what must have once been an elegantly furnished room.

Bonnie rushed to her father and threw her arms around him. "Oh, Daddy, are you okay? Did he hurt you?" She glanced around at the destruction in the room.

"I didn't touch him," the animal roared. "I'm not what you think I am."

Bonnie turned her head to look at the beast. For the briefest moment her fear gave way to astonished curiosity. There was something so odd, so pitiful about the creature's need to defend himself. He looked back at her with a peculiar expression, neither entirely human nor entirely wild.

"No, you're just a bully," Bonnie's father said. "A big, strong, spoiled child who takes what he wants and has to have everything his way and throws a very dangerous fit when he doesn't get it. A beast who has to take prisoners for lack of friends."

Bonnie could hear the low, disgruntled roar starting up deep in the beast's huge chest. His small eyes flashed dangerously. "Daddy, hush," she warned her father.

Her father only shook his head. "He won't harm us. At least not physically. But he won't let us go, either. Bonnie. Oh, Bonnie, why did you come? Now you're a prisoner in this place, too."

Bonnie spun to face the beast. "Is that true? Are you going to keep us here?"

The beast shook his huge, furry head slowly. "Not forever. No. Just until— Only as long as—" He seemed to be grappling for an excuse. "Only till I *know* that my secret is safe. That nobody will ever find out who lives inside these walls."

"I gave you my word," Bonnie's father said. "What more can I give you?"

The beast's sharp-eyed gaze was trained on Bonnie. She formed the uncomfortable realization that he hadn't let her out of his sight for a second, since he'd pulled open his door. Her father must have seen it, too.

"Give you my daughter? For my freedom? Oh, no! Never!" he exclaimed. "First you'd have to tear me apart, as you did to this room."

The beast dropped to all fours and made a slow circle around Bonnie. Bonnie felt every fiber in her body go tense—until she heard the soft purring coming from the beast. It wasn't the sound of a creature about to attack.

"Well, then," the beast finally said, "I guess you'll both be visiting with me for a while."

"Visiting! You mean we're both prisoners," Bonnie's father cried.

Were her eyes playing tricks on her? Did Bonnie actually see the beast wince? Or had a biting flea gotten into his fur? In a flash Bonnie saw that he was really something like an overgrown cat or a mammoth-sized dog. And her fright began to ebb away again, replaced by anger.

"No, he's not going to keep us both here," she said commandingly. "If I stay with you, beast, will you let my father go?"

Her father let out a choked cry. "No, Bonnie! I won't allow it!"

"Daddy, better one prisoner than two," she said as bravely as she could. Why, her father couldn't even find his way to the highway, let alone find a way to escape from this beast's lair. If anyone had to stay, she should be the one.

"You would do that?" the beast asked, scratching the top of his furry head. "You would give up your own freedom to set your father free?"

The beast's question only strengthened Bonnie's resolve. "Of course I would," she said simply. "I love him."

The beast looked from Bonnie to her father and back again. He was mewing in a forlorn way.

But Bonnie's father's words caused the beast to fall silent. "He doesn't know about love, Bonnie. He told me so himself. He's just a miserable, lonely beast."

Suddenly the beast let out a frightening roar. Bonnie jumped away from him. But her father didn't budge. "And don't even talk of staying here without me, Bonnie. I won't hear of it."

The beast reared onto his hind legs again, towering over Bonnie and her father. "Oh, but I think you will," he said. "I think it's an excellent idea."

Bonnie's fear took hold once more. Alone with this monster? Why had she said anything? Why hadn't she kept silent? But before she even had a chance to protest, the beast was grabbing her father, teeth sunk into his leather belt, and dragging him away.

"Oh, no!" Bonnie screamed. "Daddy! Daddy!" She ran behind them.

The beast hit a button with his huge paw, and the front door opened. He tossed her father outside as easily as a piece of crumpled-up paper. Her father scrambled to his feet and tried to get back in the door, but the beast blocked his way.

"Go, Daddy, go!" Bonnie yelled from inside. "My bicycle's right on the ground, over there."

"I'll get help, Bonnie! You won't be here for long!"

"You won't do anything," the beast roared. "Not if you want me to take good care of your beautiful daughter. Do you hear me, Tony?" He gave her father a push, and he tumbled under the latticework archway and off the low front step.

"Dad! Daddy!" Bonnie watched him get to his feet again. But then the beast threw his weight against the door, and it swung shut. Her father was gone from view.

And Bonnie was trapped.

Seven

"I'll escape," Bonnie swore as she faced the beast. "And at least my father is on his way home."

The beast slunk across the glass-walled oval room and hopped up onto a deep, cushioned chair. "Can't you forget about him for a few seconds?" he whimpered. "This is your new room. What do you think of it? I bet you've never had a room like this in your life."

Bonnie looked around at her windowed prison. It was a study in sleek design, and it was comfortably decorated, too, with a huge bed, a good reading lamp, and soft rugs on the polished wood floor.

The beast pressed a button on the wall, and part of the wall slid open, revealing a huge screen and a control console. "And here's your entertainment center. TV and VCR. Computer. Any movie you want, any video game, you just type in the information and hit enter. Someone will bring it up. Oh, and there's a catalog in the computer of all the books in my library, too. They're yours for the asking. And if there are any you don't see . . . well, we can get those, too." He sounded like an excited child showing off a fancy toy. *What a strange creature he is,* Bonnie thought.

Any book she wanted? Any movie? Bonnie had to admit that it sounded good. She moved toward the curve of windows. The view was breathtaking. The sun was a fiery ball sinking into the ocean. The sky and water were streaked with pink and orange, spreading into purple at the far edges of the panorama. Through the windows on the other side of the room, a sliver of moon and a lone star were already visible in the dark blue sky over the mountains. Bonnie could even see the little harbor of Land's End down the coast. She prayed her father would get there quickly and safely.

Suddenly the view meant very little. Her father was out there and she was here—captive to a talking beast. It wasn't even possible. It couldn't be real. And yet here she was, and she knew she wasn't dreaming.

The beast, curled up in his chair, followed her every movement. "Well?" he asked.

"What do I think?" Bonnie asked. She sank down on the edge of the bed. "I think this is the most beautiful prison I've ever been in."

The beast leaped off the chair and snarled. "You're just like him, aren't you? Just like your father. Don't you realize how much more luxurious this is than your puny house with the big trees in the yard?"

Bonnie's surprise was mixed with alarm. "How do you know about my house?" she asked. "And how did you know who I was when I came to the door?" What kind of inhuman powers did this beast have? Bonnie wondered.

The beast gave a peculiar snort. "It's not so difficult to find out about a person. Oh, you wouldn't believe it from the way he was carrying on before—as if I weren't any better than those wolves I saved him from—but your father and I, we got to talking. And you're going to find out, as he did, that I'm not such a bad beast to talk to, either, Bonnie."

"The wolves?" Bonnie asked. "What wolves?"

The beast's huge chest puffed up even bigger. "Well, you wouldn't know it from the things he was saying, but I saved your father's life, Bonnie."

Could it be true? Should she really be grateful to this beast?

"Oh, but I'll tell you all about it at dinner," the beast said. "There's so much to arrange, so much to prepare." He took a few four-footed steps across the floor, lumbering like an animal. Then he stopped, looked at Bonnie, and rose up on his hind legs. He crossed the rest of the room on two feet, with his head high. "You won't be sorry you stayed behind. It's going to be quite a special dinner, you'll see."

What Bonnie saw was a thin trickle of saliva at one corner of the beast's mouth. Grateful? No way. She was repulsed. "You can keep me here, but you can't force me to enjoy myself."

The beast roared. "I invite you to dine with me, and you respond that way? How dare you?"

"How dare I?" Bonnie retorted. "You didn't *invite* me to do anything at all. You told me. You ordered me. You know, there's a boy in Land's End who's a lot like you." Bonnie thought about the way Gary had tried to bully her into a date. "Yeah, Gary's pretty much of a beast, too," she mused.

"Gary," the beast snarled. "I'll make you forget all about your silly, powerless Gary. You'll see. Now I have to get everything set for dinner. Push this button—the one right here over the headboard—if there's anything you want. Anything.

I'll send someone to bring you down at half past seven."

The beast stepped out of the room and shut the door. Bonnie could hear the key turn in the lock. *Anything,* she thought. *Anything, that is, except to get out of this place.*

"Everything has to be perfect," the beast ordered his servants. "Gerard, how's the meat you just got in your weekly shipment?"

"Very tender," Gerard said, his towering white chef's toque bobbing like a balloon on top of his head as he nodded. "Nice in a garlic and red wine sauce, I think."

"Yes, that sounds delicious. But remember— Italian, yes? Don't go getting too French on me tonight. My guest will have her entree medium-rare—just a little pink inside. And I—"

"Will have it *bleu*. Bloody, yes, of course," Gerard finished for him. "In fact, I won't bother cooking it at all for you."

The beast was sure he heard one of the other servants stifle a laugh. He whirled on the rest of his staff, gathered in the kitchen at his orders. "Is there someone here who finds my pitiful predicament so amusing? Perhaps that person would like to be my dinner."

With a growl he turned back to Gerard. "We'll start with your special mushrooms, and then for dessert . . . let's see, a trio, I think. Raspberry ricotta cheesecake—do you have fresh raspberries? Something chocolate, and a sorbet to end the meal. Show me you're earning that wad of money my parents left you."

Gerard sneered. "I earn it every day, locked up in this beast's cave, seeing what you have become," he said. "How I long for the day I can go out into the world again—"

"Silence!" roared the beast. "You may leave right now—and without your money, if you long for freedom so badly. Isn't your kitchen furnished with the very latest, very best equipment? Don't you order the finest ingredients from all over the globe? Don't you have all day, every day to experiment with your culinary art?"

Gerard shook his head. "That's all there is for you—what you can buy. Perhaps you don't remember anything else. Perhaps you never learned it to begin with. But me, I wish to sit in a noisy, crowded restaurant and hear the people. Oh, and not in some computer-generated imitation, as convincing as it may be. I wish to walk all alone by the river in my hometown and maybe get lost. Or maybe meet up with a beautiful woman . . ."

When the beast heard those words, the rest of what Gerard was saying faded away. "Yes, a beautiful woman," the beast said. "There's so much to do and so little time. Now, Serafina, I want the house sparkling clean. Get that mess in the living room cleaned up."

"But won't you be dining in the dining room?" Rita put in.

The beast nodded. "But when she goes by the living room, I don't need her to be reminded of— of— Oh, why do you all insist on making this so difficult?" He wanted everything to be just right.

Bonnie! He was having dinner with Bonnie. Not some daydream of Bonnie, like he'd been having since the wolves had chased Tony to his door. Not some technologically astounding cyber-Bonnie who could accompany him to Café l'Illusion, or any of his other cyber-haunts. That would have surely followed if Bonnie herself had not come in her father's footsteps.

Fate had been cruel to this poor beast, but now he'd gotten the most wonderful break. After year upon year of living on dreams, his best dream had appeared at his door—looking even more beautiful than he'd imagined her. The clear, sparkling eyes, the soft, toffee-colored hair, the perfect face and figure. And she definitely had spirit; she definitely had fight. Yes, she had just a tiny little bit of beast in her. Truly his perfect match.

The beast purred. He was going to have to make certain the fight wasn't directed at him—show her there really was nothing to miss down in her little nothing town.

"The illusion must be flawless tonight!" he ordered. "Is someone fixing that computer hardware in the living room?"

Rita nodded. "We've got a man working on it. You chewed up some of those wires pretty badly."

"He has one hour," the beast roared. "No more than that. And Arno, let's practice. When you bring the young lady her dinner, what do you say?"

Arno rolled his dark eyes toward the ceiling. "You know I studied the foreign-language modules right along with you," he said. "You don't have to test me as if I were your student in school."

"Yes, but your accent never was as good as mine," the beast replied. "Now say it. Go through the whole routine."

Arno sighed. "Okay, say I'm bringing her an *insalata mista*. I put it down in front of her—like this. And I say, '*Prego, signorina*.'"

"Didn't you hear me, you fool? She's having

the braised wild-mushroom salad to start. Not an *insalata mista*."

Arno shrugged. "All right. I put down her mushroom salad. Her *insalata di funghi,* okay? It doesn't change what I say to her. Besides, what if she doesn't want the mushrooms?"

"It's the best appetizer for the meal."

Rita put a hand on the beast's arm. She was the only one who ever touched him, and her touch was warm on his fur. "What Arno's trying to say is that you can't order the young lady to have a perfect evening, you know?"

The beast shook away Rita's hand. His blood ran too fast. His adrenaline pumped hard. "You all want her to hate me!" he roared wildly. "You want me to remain a beast forever. As punishment for making you stay here with me all these years."

"No," Rita said. "That couldn't be further from the truth, Peter."

Peter. The beast inhaled and then let his breath out slowly.

"But don't you see that the beast is inside you?" Rita continued. "If that doesn't change, you won't, either. You have to treat the young lady with respect and kindness."

"Then what am I supposed to do?" the beast asked with a little whimper.

"First of all," Gerard jumped in, "stop thinking you can buy your way to a romantic dinner. It can't work."

The beast's whimper turned into a snarl. "I bought you, didn't I? Or my parents bought you for me. So you just do what you're told. You make the finest dinner you've ever made. One that's better than anything she's ever had in her entire life in that backward town. And I'll make it special. You'll see. You'll all see. She'll dine with me and she'll love it! It will be as perfect as—"

The beast had a flash of his rose and the petals that were slowly falling off. "As a rose in bloom," he added with less force. "She'll love it. She'd better. I don't have any other hope."

Eight

The beast, sitting in his living room armchair, was dressed in a tuxedo and a black bow tie, a white carnation in his lapel. A wild beast in a tux. *What kind of freak creature is this?* Bonnie wondered as one of the servants brought her into the large room.

"Hello," he said, getting to his feet. And for a fleeting moment Bonnie thought he actually sounded a little shy and nervous. Ha! Shy and nervous? He was her jailer. She was his captive.

"Hello," she responded icily. "I'm sorry I'm not in my evening wear, too, but I'm afraid this is all I have. You see, I didn't pack for getting trapped by a beast with a taste for fashion."

The beast surveyed her thoroughly. Sweatpants, old sweater with the hole in one elbow, sneakers covered with mud and dried leaves from the hike up the mountain—Bonnie could feel the beast taking it in. The beast shook his head. "You look beautiful just as you are," he said. "But I must admit, I imagined you in something a bit more—appropriate."

"Appropriate? For being held prisoner?" Bonnie asked.

The beast seemed to bite back a growl or a snarl. "An oversight on my part," he said, ignoring her words. He was silent for a few moments, and then he let out a bright little bark. "But I think I have a solution you may actually enjoy! Do you like to go shopping, Bonnie?" he asked.

"Shopping? Does that mean we're getting out of here?" Bonnie asked eagerly. Maybe this was her chance for escape.

"Yes and no," answered the beast. "But you do like to shop, don't you?"

Bonnie shrugged. This was so very strange. Here she was, imprisoned by a beast dressed like a man at a fancy ball, talking about shopping. What did he want with her, this strange creature? Could it be that he was as desperately lonely as her father had said?

"I don't know. I guess I like shopping as much as the next girl," Bonnie said guardedly. "But there aren't all that many places to go around Land's End. A few stores in town. A couple of department stores in the mall. There are a few really nice little boutiques that are open in the summer—you know, for the tourists, mostly. But they're awfully expensive."

"Well, where would you go if you could shop anywhere?" the beast asked. It almost seemed as if a smile was playing at the corners of his animal mouth. "And if price was no object. No object at all."

"Anywhere?" Bonnie asked. She remembered how only a few days ago—oh, so much had happened, it seemed like weeks—she'd been daydreaming about fashionable Milanese ladies sipping cappuccino.

"Anywhere," the beast confirmed.

"Well, Italy, maybe. When you see them in the movies and magazines and stuff, the women always look so stylish and poised."

The beast let out an excited little bark. "Oh, this evening really is going to be perfect! How did you know we were going to Italy for dinner, my most special guest?"

"Italy!" Bonnie felt a thrill of excitement despite herself. Despite the fact that she was captive to this strange creature. "We're going to Italy for dinner? Is that true?"

"Well, yes and no," the beast repeated again.

"Yes and no? What does that mean?"

The beast got out of his chair and moved to Bonnie's side. She resisted the impulse to move away, afraid of angering him. "Via Sognare," the beast said commandingly. "The street of dreams."

And suddenly Bonnie's fear of him dissolved into pure amazement as the walls themselves seemed to give way. The room was changing, re-shaping itself somehow, turning into . . . a bustling, tree-lined avenue teeming with people and shops and cafés. "Panetteria la Torta Impossibile" read the sign above a little store whose windows beck-oned with breads and baked goods. "Calzolaio Speroni" said the sign on the shop next door. A woman was coming out the door holding a pair of newly resoled boots. A procession of cars drove down the street—most of them far smaller than what Bonnie was used to seeing. Smaller, but noisy. One car let out a long, high blast of its horn.

"I can't believe it!" Bonnie breathed. "We're really in Italy!" She knew it must be some kind of illusion, but it seemed so real. "What is this? Like a virtual-reality machine, or something?"

"It's better if you don't think about that," the beast answered. "*Benvenuto in Italia*," he added.

"And if I'd said I'd wanted to shop in Japan? Or Brazil?" Bonnie asked incredulously.

The beast laughed. Yes, that raspy sound *was* a laugh. "There will be lots of time for that, my lovely Bonnie."

Lots of time. Bonnie was suddenly reminded that she was a prisoner. At the beast's mercy, no matter how marvelous or magical a prison she was in. And she felt a wave of longing for the smell of the ocean and the sound of the gulls, and for the ordinary house she shared with her father.

The beast didn't seem to notice her change of heart. "Shall we?" he asked happily, and he even put his arm out, as if Bonnie might touch a beast like him. "There's a wonderful little dress shop up the block. *Una notte incantata.*" Somehow the beast managed to make the fluid syllables of Italian roll easily off his thick tongue. But Bonnie wasn't going to let herself be impressed. "It means 'an enchanted night,'" the beast translated for her.

"Enchanted because it's not real," Bonnie shot back. "Not this street or the people on it. And certainly not your idea that I'm your special guest."

The beast was absolutely silent and still. He blinked his beady eyes. Was that a tear? But no. Suddenly he let out a roar that Bonnie felt right through the soles of her muddy sneakers. "You wanted to come here. You told me yourself. If you could go shopping anyplace in the world . . . And I made it happen. *I* did. Do you hear me?"

Bonnie stared at the beast curiously. He was big and powerful. His roar could rock the walls. His very word could turn his home into a wonderful, foreign place. But he was like a boy who had never quite grown up. A spoiled child. Spoiled and lonely. Bonnie sighed. "Okay, beast. Let's see what they have in your dress store, okay?" She could see she didn't have much of a choice.

And besides, the smell of freshly baked bread hung in the air. She could feel the roundness of old paving stones under her feet. A man sang in Italian as he rode down the street on a motorbike. A beautiful woman drank a glass of red wine at an outdoor café. And Bonnie had never been in Italy before. She wasn't going to take the beast's furry arm. No way. But she let him lead her down the street of this faraway town.

Maybe it wasn't going to be as hard as he'd thought to break the evil spell, the beast decided. Bonnie was so lovely, sitting opposite him in her midnight blue silk shift and the azure teardrop-shaped earrings he'd bought to go with it. He didn't know why she'd wanted that other dress so badly, the deep red one with the matching jacket. It was nice enough, sure, but what wouldn't look great on her?

And she is as intelligent as she is beautiful, he thought as he watched her finish up her dinner. She knew about art and science and so much more. "You know where noodles were first invented?" she'd asked, turning the discussion to Marco Polo's voyage to China as she'd eaten up every bite of the capellini Gerard had prepared.

Oh, he liked her voracious appetite, almost as wild as his. And the richness with which she described the ordinary details of her life, so that the beast found them even more vivid than when her father described them.

"The pulleys make this terrible squeal when we bring the lobster pots up out of the water, and the boat sways like crazy sometimes. . . . Makes it even nicer coming inside at the end of a long day of work. Cozy, calm."

The beast could almost imagine himself free of this animal body, working the sea alongside Bonnie and then relaxing at the end of the day.

But, oh, the sad, faraway expression in her blue eyes when she talked about home. It was almost enough to make him set her free. He couldn't, though. If he did, she'd never come to see how right they were together—how they loved the same books and movies. How they dreamed of the same faraway places. How the world could be in their hands if only she would open her heart to him.

The beast lowered his face into his plate and devoured his meat. He saw Bonnie's mouth turn down in distaste. He quickly sat up and dabbed at his mouth with the corner of his cloth napkin. The last little piece of meat sat partially chewed and bloody on the fancy china. The beast put a finger up in the air, and Arno appeared immediately, wearing black pants, a white shirt, and a vest with "Ristorante Toscana" embroidered tastefully above the watch pocket.

"*Signore*, we're both finished. You may take our plates," the beast commanded.

Arno nodded. "*Dolci?* Desserts for the lady and gentleman? *Caffè?*"

"Mmm, yeah, Italian gelato," Bonnie said. "It's supposed to be the best ice cream in the world, isn't it? I want a big bowl of it. What flavors do you have?"

The beast found himself making that funny sound again, that sound that tickled his nose and throat. Laughter. She made him laugh, this beautiful girl, laugh the way he had when he was still a boy, a human. "We've got a wonderful pear sorbet," he said. "And a raspberry cheesecake, and chocolate—truffles, I think they are. The lady will have all three, plus a decaffeinated cappuccino. And one for me, too." Bonnie didn't have to know it was his usual coffee-colored disguised bowl of milk.

Arno nodded and rushed off.

"It isn't so bad, is it?" he asked Bonnie. "Having dinner with me in romantic Italy?"

But Bonnie was frowning, her eyes flashing as brightly as her jeweled earrings. "You ordered my whole meal for me. You didn't even let me pick my own dessert."

"Oh, but you'll love what he's bringing you. It's the best thing you could have asked for."

"But I didn't ask for it. Or anything else. You picked my outfit, you picked what I ate, you decided which chair I'd sit in." Her voice rose, but the diners at the next table didn't even turn around, politely ignorant cyber-creations that they were.

The beast slammed a powerful paw on the table. "I did it for you! I picked out the best because I wanted you to have the best!" He couldn't quite manage to stop the roar that followed his words the way a tail follows a dog.

Bonnie's response was quiet but furious. "If you want the best for me, then let me go. Send me back to my father, where I belong."

The beast had to use all his powers of control not to tear up the room the way he'd done earlier. "I thought you were enjoying yourself," he growled. "It certainly seemed as though you thought your dinner was good. I didn't catch you sending anything back to the kitchen. You didn't mind seeing how every dress in the store looked on you. And I even heard you practicing a few words of Italian when we stopped to watch those men playing *bocce* on our walk over here."

Bonnie let out a long sigh. "Okay, your magical mansion is pretty great. Incredible. I'll admit that. The food was delicious. Way better than at Mezzaluna, over in Oceanview. And I mean, I've always dreamed about going to Italy, and now . . ." She made a generous wave around her.

Her hand was so slender and graceful, the beast thought. He hid his huge, unsightly paws under the table.

"And now I'm here," Bonnie continued. "In Italy. Well, almost. See, that's the problem. I start to forget that this is all pretend. I start to forget I'm here because I can't leave. And then—"

"Then why can't you keep forgetting?" the beast asked. He held back a roar. He'd done everything he could to make the night perfect, hadn't he?

"Because you won't let me," Bonnie answered. "Because you tell me what to do and what to wear and what to eat. Because you order me around and make me remember that I'm at your mercy. Because you really are a beast."

Beast. Beast. Beast. Her final word rang in his ears. Yes, he had done everything he could to make the night perfect except turn himself into a handsome, human boy. This time he couldn't hold back. The roar started deep in his chest, and his whole body trembled with it. It bounced off the walls. It shook the floor. Louder and louder he roared, as loud and long as he could. Anything to drown out the sound of that horrible word in his head. *Beast.*

Nine

He was going to have her. This was his chance. Gary watched the crowd around Tony Oliviera with a growing sense of glee. Bonnie was in some sort of trouble, and Gary was going to save her. She'd never close the door on him again.

Her father waved his arms around, distraught. "She's been kidnapped. He's got her. Someone's got to help me."

The mad scientist looks loonier than ever tonight, Gary thought. His clothes were disheveled, as if he'd been sleeping in them for days. His shoes were covered with mud and leaves, and he'd ridden into town on Bonnie's bicycle, which was way too small for him and was hot pink besides. What a loser the guy was. But none of that mattered, because he was going to make Gary a winner.

"Who's this 'he'? Who's got her?" Dick Johnson asked, putting his big, greasy mitt on Tony's shoulder. "Calm down, buddy, and tell us what happened to your little girl."

"She's up in the Lair. The beast's got her," Tony said frantically.

"The beast? You mean the monster in that old myth people like to tell around here?" Dick's wife, Betty, said with a derisive laugh.

"No, he's real, and he's up there with Bonnie. He said if I told anyone . . . Oh, I've got to get her before he finds out I've given away his secret."

"Wait a minute, Tony," Dick Johnson said. "You mean this beast can talk? You're telling us your daughter's been kidnapped by a talking beast?" He opened his eyes wide and raised his eyebrows. "And you say he's holding her in the deserted mansion up on the cliff?" He mimed chugging from an invisible bottle. "You been spending a little too much time in the bar, man?"

A few cackles went around the little crowd of people. "Naw, he wasn't," said Steve Marlow, who'd come stumbling down the street a few moments before. "I was just in there having a few brewskis, and Tony wasn't around. Don't think I've ever seen him in there, actually."

If anyone would know who'd been hanging out at the Down and Under Bar, Gary thought, *it was Steve, the lush.*

"Probably just spending too much time on those cockamamy inventions," Steve went on, his words slurred. "Making him think funny, ya know?"

"No, cross my heart! The beast is real!" Tony Oliviera protested. He sounded panicky; he couldn't catch his breath. "The mansion is *not* deserted! I swear it!"

"Are you sure Bonnie didn't just take off for a while?" someone else was asking. It was that short guy who'd been in Gary's shop class the year before—what was his name? "Everyone who knows her knows she doesn't want to stick around Land's End any longer than she has to."

"Yeah, that's true," put in scrawny Eddie Talbot. "Remember her yearbook quote, Jasper?" Jasper—that was the puny guy's name. "She sure isn't planning on staying here forever. Maybe she ran away," Eddie said to the group of people around Bonnie's father.

"No, she didn't. I saw her," Bonnie's father cried. "I just came from the Lair, and the beast's got her there."

Gary noticed that his uncle Ralph had just come out of the grocery store. He crossed the street and joined the crowd, listening to what was going on.

"Wait a minute, Tony. See if you can get a grip on yourself and tell me what all this is about," Uncle Ralph ordered.

"Chief Belsky, it's my daughter," Bonnie's father said. "She's being held prisoner. We have to go rescue her."

"He says the beast's got her up in the Lair," Betty Johnson said. "He says he needs our help to get her back. And get this—he says the beast talks!" She shook her head, and all her chins wobbled. *Can't get uglier than that*, thought Gary. Boy, he wouldn't want Betty Johnson helping him, no matter what kind of hot water he'd gotten into.

"The Lair? Everyone knows that place is abandoned," Uncle Ralph stated flatly. "You have any kind of ransom note? Any proof that your daughter's missing?"

"I saw him with her, with my own eyes," Bonnie's father cried. "What further proof do I need?"

Uncle Ralph arched a skeptical eyebrow. "And she didn't tell you she was going away somewhere? Tell you maybe she was taking a little trip with a friend?"

"I saw her! Do you hear me? And I saw the beast! He's seven feet tall and hairy, with huge, sharp teeth—two rows of them! And he's got my Bonnie! My daughter's up there!"

Gary saw his uncle shake his head. He knew Uncle Ralph thought the mad scientist was a crackpot. "First *she's* saying *you're* missing, Tony. Now here *you* are, saying *she's* missing. Maybe you should start leaving each other notes once in a while. Or come up with one of those inventions of yours to keep track of where the other one is. . . ."

Gary let the conversation go on. It was easy to see why people thought Tony Oliviera was a little nuts. But Gary knew how fiercely loyal Bonnie was to the mad scientist. She'd never leave him alone. Especially not without saying a word. And besides, Gary had heard the beast's frightening roar with his own ears, the last time he'd dared Pat and Mark to go up to the Lair with him.

But Gary just stood there on the edge of the group listening. He didn't say a word. Let Bonnie get really frightened. Serve her right for rejecting him so rudely. Bring her down to size. And her father—he needed to get desperate.

And then, when things were looking most hopeless, Gary would storm in and save the day. Big hero, the works. Bonnie wouldn't turn him away then.

For breakfast Bonnie had mint tea and honeyed pastries in Morocco in a whitewashed restaurant with a keyhole-shaped door. Then it was on to visit the lovely, tranquil Rodin Museum in Paris, where his famous Thinker pondered the mysteries of the universe. Chin on his fist, elbow on his knee, he was so familiar to Bonnie from all the photos she had seen. But to walk around and examine him from any angle, to be able to follow the entire fluid curve from his head to his shoulder, down his back to his muscular legs. . . .

"It's amazing!" Bonnie said, walking around the statue once, slowly, and then again.

"Yeah, it's beautiful—so strong," the beast said. Bonnie looked over to see the curious picture of the beast studying the piece ever so carefully.

"Well, yeah, the sculpture's incredible, too," Bonnie said. "But what I really meant is that it's so amazing just to be able to see this."

"I'm glad," the beast said simply. And it sounded to Bonnie as if he really meant it. He was certainly trying his best to make her forget the wild creature who'd howled his way through dessert the night before. She'd chosen the destinations that day, and the beast had agreed to everything she'd requested. She'd been the one to put in the breakfast order—and had even found herself not wanting to spoil the illusion by pointing out that their waiter was the same one who'd served them at the Italian restaurant the night before, though now he sported a small round Muslim hat and a fake beard and mustache.

Of course, she could never forget she was a prisoner here in the Lair, could never forget that she was either locked in her room or under the watchful eye of the beast. He hadn't let her out of his sight for a second.

But strolling through the halls of this gem of a museum, Bonnie found she couldn't be entirely unhappy about being in this house of illusion, either. Venice, Hong Kong, the shores of the South Pacific—Bonnie wanted to see them all. Why, the Lair was a kind of dream machine. Or at least it would be if she could get free of the beast.

She watched him inspect a tiny statue of a man on a horse. He looked so cultured, so civilized. But Bonnie wasn't going to be fooled. "Beast," she muttered under her breath. He was the same inhuman soul keeping her under lock and key, keeping her from her home and her family.

Dad. He must be sick with worry, Bonnie thought. If only she could let him know that she was fine here in the Lair. She was lonely for home, but she had to admit that it wasn't all bad in the beast's cyber-lair.

The beast approached her, his tail dragging on the museum floor. "You look as pensive as our friend here," he said, pointing a heavy, golden-furred paw at the Thinker. "Penny for your thoughts. Or more. As much as you want. Anything you want."

Anything. Oh, sure. But Bonnie only shrugged. Why make the beast as angry as he'd gotten the night before?

"We could go talk out in the sculpture garden," the beast said. "It's so lovely. I want you to see it. Oh, but I wasn't going to order you around today. No, I'd made a promise to myself. . . ."

"We can go outside if you want," Bonnie said. "Actually, I'd like to see the garden." She tried not to give in to the tiny tickle of compassion she felt for the beast despite herself. He reminded her just a bit of one of the painfully shy boys she'd gone to school with—boys who didn't quite know how to act or talk with a girl.

And then there had been that moment at breakfast when the beast had stopped to look at and smell a brilliantly colored desert flower growing like a weed against the bright white wall of the Moroccan restaurant. And just now when he'd been studying the art in the museum with such rapt attention. . . . In these brief moments he seemed so human, so thoughtful and sensitive. Bonnie almost forgot that he was hideous to look at, that he was unnatural—and that he could rip her apart with one bite of his knife-sharp teeth.

She followed him out into the museum garden. The artist's lush, curvy, romantic statues softened the line of the stately paths and ordered plots of grass like spectacular carved white flowers. The sun hit her full in the face. She tilted her chin up to catch the warmth. It was a beautiful day.

The beast stretched like an overgrown cat. "Like it? It's one of my favorite spots."

It was hard to disagree. Bonnie nodded. A spot of tranquility within the bustling city, a garden of imagination to feed the senses.

"You know, we could have a picnic lunch out here if you want," the beast said. "I mean, it's just a suggestion. I'm not telling you we have to, okay? Normally they wouldn't allow you to do that here. But, well, since this is our own private version of Monsieur Rodin's museum, I think we can bend the rules a little. A loaf of bread, some good cheese, pâté, a simple salad . . ."

Bonnie sighed. "You want me to be a happy prisoner."

"Not a prisoner. A guest," the beast said. "I want you to feel like a guest in my house."

Bonnie sat down on the nearest bench. The stone was warm from the sun. "Then let me leave," she said to the beast.

She could hear the beast swallow a growl. "I just don't understand what's so great at home," he said. "Isn't this one of the places you've always wanted to go? Isn't this what you always dreamed about when you were trapped down in Land's End?"

"Yes and yes," Bonnie answered truthfully.

"Then what have you got there that you don't have here?" he pressed. "A boyfriend! I should have known it! Of course. It's some pretty-faced boy you're missing, isn't it?" The beast let out a disgusted snarl.

"No. There isn't anyone like that. I mean, I wish there were, but there isn't," Bonnie said.

"Then what?" the beast demanded.

"My father." Bonnie felt a stab of emptiness.

"So you don't see him for a while," the beast said, shrugging his massive shoulders. "Big deal. It's not like it's forever."

"Then when?" Bonnie said. "When are you going to let me see him again? When are you going to let me free?"

"Just until— Well, the day is coming soon when I— Oh, never mind," the beast said with a snap of his bright teeth. "Until I say you can go, is when."

Bonnie swallowed her tears. No, she couldn't let down her guard with the beast. Not for a second. Enjoy his dream machine, yes. Travel the world she'd been aching to see, yes—as long as she had to be stuck in this place. But the most important thing was to find a way out.

Because none of this was real, except for the lock on her door.

Ten

"My goodness, I haven't heard you sing in years," exclaimed Rita as she breezed into the beast's room to turn down his bedcovers. "Isn't that the silly bedtime rhyme I used to sing to you when you were small?"

The beast's face grew warm. "Yeah, I guess it is. One sheep, two sheep, pink sheep, blue sheep," he sang. For all these years he hadn't even known that he *could* sing with his beast's voice.

Rita chimed in on the last few notes, laughing brightly. "It's Bonnie. She makes you sing, Peter!"

For once it seemed right for Rita to call him by his true name. The beast felt the corners of his mouth go up. He was smiling! "She's beautiful, isn't she?" he asked Rita. "The way she looks, the way she is . . ."

Rita nodded. "Yes, she's a lovely girl. I can understand why you're growing so fond of her. But . . . Peter, how long do you think you can keep her here this way? It won't endear you to her, I can tell you that."

The beast's smile mutated into a fierce gnashing of his teeth. "Silence!" he commanded. "She didn't seem to mind being stuck in Morocco or Paris or any of the other places we visited today."

Rita shook her head sadly. "I've been silent way too long, and your time is running out, Peter. You have to banish the beast inside you, don't you see? Learn to make your fellow souls happy. Is that so difficult?"

A roar built up in the beast's powerful chest. But then he thought of Bonnie's sparkling eyes and her natural smile, and the roar died down without ever making it up through his throat. "No, it's not so awful to try to make a person happy. It's even kind of nice. Oh, Rita, when I took her for a surprise after-lunch ride in a horse and buggy around Central Park in New York City, she laughed right out loud, can you believe it? I made someone laugh! I made *Bonnie* laugh."

Bonnie and the beast, he thought. *Bonnie and . . . Peter.*

But then he caught sight of his hideous, hairy,

pointy-nosed face in his mirror. Peter? Ha. Peter was long gone.

Rita's round face was reflected alongside his. "The problem is that behind her laughter, she's still your prisoner," she said softly but firmly. "No one can live happily that way."

For many long, lonely years, Rita's face had been one of the few the beast had seen. Well, unless you counted his cyber-creations. And now, once again, he was seeing the changes all these years had wrought—the lines, the worry in her blue eyes, the gray streaking her once-blond hair. She looked tired and worried and so sad.

"You're saying that because you know the feeling firsthand," the beast said, realizing it was true. "Because you think of yourself as my prisoner, too. You *are* going to leave me when the rose dies, aren't you, Rita? Along with everybody else in this house." He let out a whimper. "Leave me in this gruesome beast's body, all by myself."

In the mirror, he saw Rita reach out toward him. She patted his paw gently. "I hope not, Peter. I hope not. But the way to the young lady's heart is not through lock and key. You have to let her go. There is no other choice."

Peter thought about Bonnie's sweet, clear

laughter. And about his own. Laughter—that simple human pleasure had been so long buried he'd forgotten how vital it was. Let go of the girl who could make that happen?

Rita was wrong. She didn't understand. She didn't know what it was like to live in this hateful monster's skin. And if he let Bonnie go, he'd be doomed to it forever. He'd never smile or sing again.

Gary moved closer to Jan Wilson in the booth at Dairy Dream. They sat on the same side of the table, a chocolate sundae melting, uneaten, in front of them. It was a small price to pay for what he wanted.

"You know Bonnie thought she was too good for Land's End," Gary said, his face inches away from Jan's. "And now she's out of here, and her father just can't deal."

"Yeah, now she's out of here," Jan echoed happily. She stared up at Gary with big, adoring brown eyes.

Gary held her gaze and lowered his voice in an intimate way. "Can you keep a secret?"

Jan nodded eagerly. Gary held back a snicker. Everyone knew Jan was gossip central among the Land's End High crowd. In fact, Gary was counting on it.

"Well, I even heard that a few people saw her getting on the bus down the coast with a huge backpack," he told her confidentially. "But don't say anything, okay? I mean, it would hurt the loony old man so bad to be reminded that she packed up without even saying good-bye to him."

"My lips are sealed," Jan said.

Right. For about thirty seconds, Gary thought. "Good," he said out loud, brushing her eager, talkative lips with his. *Mmm.* Jan was a pretty good kisser. He drew her in for seconds. Her silky chestnut-colored hair smelled sweet and fresh.

"Gary," she murmured, kissing him back hungrily.

"Jan," he whispered back.

But in his head he was whispering, *Bonnie.* Soon *she* would be kissing him this way.

Bonnie had traveled the globe that day, but she was still trapped in the tower of the Lair. Memories of her picnic in the Parisian museum faded to an old dream as she worked an unbent paper clip in the keyhole of her door. She wiggled it up and down. She pushed it and jiggled it. But with just a bit too much pressure, the thin metal wire finally doubled back on itself uselessly.

"Darn!" she muttered.

Bonnie had tried everything she could think of. Slipping a credit card from her wallet into the space between the door and the door frame, trying to open the lock with it, the way she'd seen it done on TV. Opening one of the windows wide to see if there was any way to make it safely to the ground. Checking heating vents and praying one of them might prove to be an escape tunnel. But there seemed to be no way out of this room.

"Forget it. Just forget it," she said to herself. She threw the crumpled paper clip down on the floor in disgust. She flopped onto her bed. She could watch a movie to pass the time—any movie at all that was out on video. She could read a book. She could listen to music on the fancy stereo system, or watch TV on a huge screen. She could press one of the buttons on the wall above the bed and order up anything from a snack to a real feast.

But how could she enjoy any of that when all she could think about was getting out of here? She got back up and paced the room. There had to be some way to escape from this place. She needed to come up with a plan. She went over to the window and stared out at the velvety dark ocean way below her, split by a stream of light from the hazy moon.

It could have been the most exciting day she'd had in—well, ever. Morocco, Paris, a ride all around New York City's Central Park in an old-fashioned horse and buggy . . . The beast knew so much about all the places they visited and everything they were seeing. She had to admit that he was an excellent tour guide.

But each time she'd begun to lose herself in travel and adventure, something would remind her of her father. And then the curtain of fantasy would come tumbling down. She'd notice that the beast's servant Arno was driving their horse and carriage. Or that the beast's jeans and shirt barely covered up his true form. Then the computer-driven nature of the illusion became impossible to ignore.

In the museum that day Bonnie had even bumped right into a man who was looking at Rodin's the Kiss without his noticing a thing.

"Oh, excuse me!" she'd said automatically.

But the man had simply continued along on his preprogrammed track, stroking his beard as he studied the art.

Still, it would have been so easy to ignore the edge of disbelief if Bonnie had really wanted to. If she hadn't been cyber-traveling as the beast's prisoner. True, for a few moments here and there she'd been so swept up in the thrill of new places that she'd almost forgotten the real situation. And there had even been a few moments when the beast had seemed to forget himself, too, and show a part of himself that seemed—well, human.

But in the end it always came back to the same thing. Bonnie couldn't leave the Lair. She pressed her palm to the smooth, cool glass of the window. The real world was right outside—only she couldn't get to it.

In fairy tales, the perfect man would come to save her. He'd come racing up the hill and right into the Lair. The beast would look at him and know he'd met his match. And Bonnie would look at him and know she'd found the man of her dreams. Sensitive, adventurous, handsome, smart . . . Bonnie let out a forlorn sigh. And here she was, locked up with a beast.

Down in the Land's End harbor, a few lights twinkled like stars—people working on their boats after night had fallen, or going out for an early-summer sail in the sultry night. Was her father there, alone on the deck of the *Bonita II,* worried, miserable, wondering what he could do? Was he brooding in their lonely, empty house?

Bonnie felt her eyes filling with tears. *Oh, Daddy, when will I see you again?* she cried silently. *When will I ever get back to Land's End?*

Eleven

There was a polite knock on the door. "Bonnie?" the beast's voice called out. Bonnie turned a teary-eyed face to the sound. As if she could really open the door from the inside and let him in.

"Yeah," she replied listlessly, not getting out of the chair she'd been sitting in since she woke up. In the bright, new light of the day, she could watch the boats going in and out of the Land's End harbor and picture the familiar rhythms of the morning in her town. The regulars would be sitting around the Foghorn, nursing bottomless cups of coffee. Maybe a few of them would have their kids in tow, since it was the weekend. Vendors would be setting up for the flea market in the baseball field behind the elementary school. People would be pulling up to Porter's News to buy their paper. She and her father would probably be out on the water already if she weren't locked up here in this high-tech prison.

She heard the rattle of a key in her door. It opened, and there stood the beast, dressed casually in a pair of jeans and a polo shirt. "Good morning." He gave her an awkward smile, as if he couldn't quite do it with his animal face, or as if he'd perhaps forgotten how it was done.

"Good morning, beast," Bonnie said dully.

"Bonnie, why are you sitting there when there are so many adventures we could be having?" he asked. "Where would you like to go today?"

"Home to my father," Bonnie said.

The smile turned into a growl. "No matter how hard I try, it's not enough for you. I meant, where would you like to go with *me?*"

Bonnie shrugged. "What does it matter where we go? At the end of the day, you'll throw me back in here and lock me in."

The beast took a few leaping strides to Bonnie's side. She could hear the frightening sounds low in his throat as he circled her chair on all four paws. The wild beast sizing up his prey. But then he stopped, looked at her for a long moment, and laid himself down at the foot of her chair like a faithful pet of some sort. "Well, would you like to stay in your room all day?" he asked quietly, sadly. "There are so many incredible things we could do. Have you ever wanted to visit the Acropolis in Greece?"

Bonnie felt an unplanned glimmer of enthusiasm. She didn't want to give the beast the satisfaction of seeing it, but the lure of traveling the world was so strong. "The ruins of Greece! Well, it would be a lie if I said I didn't want to see them." She kept her tone cool.

"Ruins, or the way it was back when ancient Greece was in its prime?" the beast asked.

"What? You mean we can go back in time, too?" She couldn't keep the excitement out of her voice now.

"Well, you realize it's a recreation according to the best of our historians' knowledge," the beast said. "And of course they don't know everything. Especially the further back you go. So it's a simulation. Like an educated guess, you know? But a pretty amazing one, I've found from the trips I've made. Venice when it was new, Victorian London . . ."

Bonnie felt a wave of hunger. "Spain in the early part of the century? Do you have a program for that?"

"Hemingway? Matadors? *Death in the Afternoon?*"

"Oh, you even know the name of the book I was thinking about!" Bonnie said with shock. She remembered Gary Belsky's lame joke about "this Matty guy" the night he had come to her house. Okay, so maybe Gary was even more of an uncivilized beast than the beast.

"One of my favorites," the beast replied. "Though I have to say, I just can't seem to help rooting for the bull, the poor, ill-fated beast."

Oh, no, thought Bonnie, *he's doing it again*. This huge, angry, ugly beast—this creature who had her locked away—was somehow almost managing to make her forget all of that.

"Yeah, I think we have a program for the sunny Spain you're thinking about," he said.

Bonnie hesitated. But only for a moment. "Okay," she agreed. "Then let's visit Hemingway's Spain today. But don't think for a second this means I'm your special guest."

Thank you, Jan Wilson, Gary thought.

His foot hard on the gas pedal, he drove quickly and purposefully toward Bonnie's house. By now it was all over town how Bonnie had left Land's End with her bags packed. Gary's friend who ran a charter fishing boat told him that not even the guys down at the harbor really believed

Tony Oliviera's story anymore. They'd been making beast sounds behind his back for days and saying that this time he'd flipped for good.

Gary's truck bounced over the cracks and potholes the winter storms had left. Too bad about Jan. He hadn't returned any of her phone calls since their "date." Not that she was a slouch in the looks department, either. But she wasn't Bonnie.

Bonnie, the beautiful captive. Bonnie, the beast's prisoner, whom Gary was going to save. Gary smiled slyly to himself. It wasn't as if he hoped the beast had hurt her. No, but maybe he'd scared her enough so that Bonnie would be wildly grateful when Gary broke down the door to the Lair.

Gary turned into the Olivieras' dirt driveway. Oh, Bonnie was going to beg him to rescue her. And when she was properly sorry for having treated him so rudely, he'd take her in his arms and get his reward.

Gary turned his engine off and hopped out of his truck. The door to the house was open, so he let himself in. He found Bonnie's father sitting at his kitchen table, just staring off into space miserably. He had the beginnings of a beard, as if he hadn't shaved since Bonnie disappeared. He looked as if he hadn't slept, either. Tony barely reacted when Gary appeared before him.

"Don't you believe in knocking?" he asked, clearly not caring much at all. "What are you doing here, young man?"

Gary sat down at the table with him. "Let's talk about how we're going to get your daughter back from that beast."

Bonnie's father sat up straight. "You believe me? I thought all you kids from school thought I was nuts."

"You must have heard about some other kids," Gary said, assuming his most sincere-sounding voice. "Me, I've heard the beast up there in the Lair myself."

The mad scientist looked grateful for this bit of confirmation. "You have?"

Gary nodded. "His roar sent me packing about as fast as I could go."

"You know, I was starting to think that pretty soon I'd be convinced this whole thing was a nightmare I'd had and somehow started believing," Bonnie's father said.

Gary shook his head. "No, pretty soon everyone will know the truth. And this time I don't intend to be scared off by a roar or two. Not when the beast's got your daughter in there. Pretty soon we're going to have Bonnie back where she belongs."

"I'd be eternally grateful," her father said. "And so would she."

Gary felt a beat of satisfaction. "That's what I'm counting on," he said. "You just make sure that she is."

"Anything to save my daughter," Tony Oliviera said. "Oh, Bonnie, Bonnie . . . if it hadn't been for me, none of this would have happened."

"Then it's your responsibility to help me get her back," Gary said. "I want you to tell me everything that's happened so far. Everything you know about the beast and the Lair. And then leave it up to me. Soon your daughter's going to be safe and in my hands."

"Go ahead," the beast encouraged Bonnie. "It only looks like sherry. You know, because that's the thing they're all drinking in this place. But it's really apple cider they poured in your glass." He pushed the tiny, tulip-shaped glass of golden liquid across the rough wooden table toward her. Through the open doorway, Bonnie saw a horse and wagon go by, clacking and clattering over the cobblestones.

All around the room, just below the ceiling, were rows of dark, heavy sherry barrels tapped with brass spigots. A long counter displayed tray upon tray of delicious foods for snacking, from a fluffy potato omelette cut into small wedges, to a salad of miniature clams, to strips of deep red roasted peppers and marinated black olives. Bonnie had ordered several tiny plates of different dishes.

Bonnie took a small taste from her glass. The cider was sweet and slightly sparkling. "And yours? Is that the real thing that you have in there?" She watched the beast take a sip of his drink, holding the stem of the glass precariously between both paws.

The beast leaned across the table toward her conspiratorially. "I'll let you in on a secret, but you have to promise not to laugh. I'm drinking milk out of this sherry glass."

"Milk!" Bonnie exclaimed, much too loudly. The tiny place was packed with people after the bullfight—senoritas with large lacy shawls draped around their shoulders, men parrying in the air with invisible swords as they dissected every move the matador had made, young people, old people, everyone in town. But no one turned to look as Bonnie's voice rang out in the small room. Still, the beast hung his big head and studied the table.

"I'm sorry, but I can't help thinking it's kind of funny," Bonnie said. "This big, tough beast with a sherry glass of milk." *This big, tough beast who keeps me away from my home,* she thought, with less amusement.

"And have you ever heard of a beast who drinks sherry?" he defended himself.

Bonnie couldn't stop herself from laughing. "So you're really just a big pussycat with your glass of milk? I mean, I saw how shaky you were when the matador went for that bull."

"Well, the only reason you noticed me was because you couldn't look at what was going on in the ring yourself," the beast tossed back.

"Ugh," Bonnie agreed. "I know it's supposed to be like an art or something. I could sort of understand it when I was reading about it in that book. But when I actually saw it . . . I just can't believe people go to these things for fun. I kept having to remind myself that it wasn't real—that it was all this super-duper hologram kind of thing created by all your magic machines." She popped an olive into her mouth, savoring the rich, salty flavor.

The beast chuckled. "Well, I guess there *is* an

up side to the fact that it's just a simulation. That poor beast of a bull in there is just a bunch of pixels and impressive electronic pyrotechnics."

Bonnie nodded slowly, watching a young couple carrying their drinks past her to a rear table. If she stuck her foot in their path, they wouldn't stumble. They wouldn't spill a drop of what was in their glasses. They'd just continue along their preprogrammed path. Bonnie sighed. She'd had an amazing day. Yes, she had, in spite of the beast. But all of this was only as real as she let it be.

"Don't you ever wish you could visit the genuine places?" she found herself asking the beast. "I mean, in a way, doesn't such a great—what did you call it?—simulation just whet your appetite for the real thing? You couldn't go back in time, but southern Spain, Paris, the Italian countryside—those places exist. They're out there right now."

The beast's rough growl caught Bonnie by surprise. She gave a frightened jump in her seat. "See?" the beast said, leaning his huge form back in the crude wooden chair. "How can I go anywhere at all? I've even scared you. I'm a beast. A monster. Can you imagine what people would do if they saw me having a drink in a little place like this in their town? The crowd would clear out faster than you could yell 'Fire!' That is, if they didn't kill me first. I'd be sort of like that bull that's doomed to die."

Bonnie couldn't help it. She felt sorry for the beast.

"No, I can never leave the boundaries of my fancy house again," he continued miserably. "Not in this body. No way. Not the way it is now," he lamented.

"The way it is now? You mean it once was different? I mean—oh, my gosh—you once were . . ." Bonnie felt the shocking realization taking hold.

"A boy," the beast confirmed. "Once upon a time I was a human being, just like you."

Bonnie looked at his black talonlike nails, his tiny animal eyes, the slit of a mouth under the black pad of a nose. "B-But . . . h-how?" she stammered. His huge, furry body was impossible to conceal, even under his well-made, human-style clothes. How had this freak of nature come to be?

The beast drew a sip of his sherry-tinted milk. "It's a long story. An awful story. But what it comes down to is this: I acted like a beast and I became a beast." He closed his little beady eyes. "Rita's told me exactly that. More than once.

And the rest of my house staff, well, they just love to throw it in my face, too. But me, I've never been able to admit it out loud before now. I mean, why should I? What good would it do? Who would even care?"

Bonnie felt another tug of sympathy for the beast. She could hardly believe the words she heard coming out of her own mouth. "Back there at the bullfights . . . when you were rooting for that poor bull? Well, I almost forgot that you were a beast. I've almost forgotten more times than I wanted to let on," she said.

"Almost. Almost. But then you look at my gruesome, unnatural face."

Bonnie shook her head. "No, then I think about my father. About the lock on the door of the room upstairs. And how that's what's real. Not all the cyber-magic, as dazzling as it is."

The beast was silent. Bonnie followed his gaze to the single rose in a narrow-necked white clay jug at the end of the bar. The beautiful pink rose that was everywhere they traveled to. A dewy petal lay on the varnished but pitted bar.

"Well, would you feel differently if you weren't here as . . . a prisoner?" the beast finally said softly, his gaze returning to Bonnie's face. "Would you think that I was any less of a . . . beast?"

Bonnie shrugged. Could she forget about his terrible roar? His deadly fangs? His furry, pointed face? She had seen little flashes of a human soul deep inside this creature, true. But when he threw her in her room and locked the door, he was nothing but a beast.

"But if I didn't hold you here, you'd leave," he whimpered like a dog that needed petting.

Bonnie was hesitant to lie. The poor beast. To be a boy once, and now to be this. No wonder he behaved so badly. Still, given the chance, she knew she'd run from these prison walls as fast as she could. Flee to her father before the beast changed his mind. She quashed an ember of guilt. She owed the beast nothing. He'd taken her freedom, this sad, spoiled house pet. And she was going to take it back.

"No, I won't go," she said, her fingers crossed under the thick wooden table. "We're getting to be friends, aren't we, beast? So if you want me to stay awhile and be your guest, I will."

The beast gave a smile so human, Bonnie almost went back on her lie. Almost. But she wasn't going to live with "almost" anymore. Exotic places that were almost real. A beast who was almost human. Her feeling almost sorry for him. And she darn sure wasn't going to stick around as a prisoner here when her chance for escape finally came.

"I promise you, it won't be forever," the beast said as he had before. "Not unless you want it to be."

She watched his eyes go toward the rose again. Somewhere, in the back of her mind, she wondered what that flower meant, and what connection it had to the beast's words. But she was too busy plotting her nighttime escape to ask. The very next day she would be in Land's End again. She'd be free.

Twelve

"Peter. Peter Crowley." The beast tried the old familiar syllables of his name out on his thick, clumsy animal tongue. *How do you do? I'm Peter Crowley, nice to meet you.*

He could almost imagine his heavy burden of fur falling away to reveal the smooth, tender skin of a human, his pointy, frightening face shrinking back to its former dimensions, his body stretching long and lean and upright, so that he could walk with his head held high.

She was his friend! Bonnie was here because she wanted to be. The beast did a little dance around his room, his huge body feeling unusually light. Oh, to go down to the beach again and jump the ocean waves, to stroll crowded streets—real ones with real people. To be free! If Bonnie could make him human again, what wonderful adventures they could have.

He pictured them starting off on a cruise around the globe: a boat just big enough to navigate the open sea but cozy enough for two, a send-off at the Land's End harbor, Bonnie's father breaking a champagne bottle on the side of the boat and making a toast.

"To smooth sailing on the sea of love," he might say.

Tony Oliviera would be master of the Lair, adding his inventions to the magic of the house, while the beast and Bonnie were on their voyages. Bonnie would be on deck, one hand on the ship's topside steering wheel, the other hand waving good-bye, salt wind blowing through her toffee-colored hair. The beast—no, Peter—would be by her side, navigational map in one slender, nimble, human hand, and a compass in the other. No simple push of the button for an adventure as rich and complicated as real life.

The beast let out a very human-sounding sigh. And what kind of couple would he and Bonnie make as they pulled out of the harbor? What would he look like by her side once he was a human, a man? Tall and imposing, with a mop of fair, curly hair like his long-ago images of his father? Strong and graceful and regal-looking, like his mother? Would Bonnie like the lines and curves of his face? Would she find him as handsome in his new form as he was hideous in this one?

Might she raise her long, elegant fingers to his face and let him feel the tenderness of her touch? The beast was filled with a joy he had long ago forgotten. The ocean around them, nothing but open possibilities in all directions . . . might she raise her perfect, full lips to him, seeking the warmth of his loving kiss?

Sinking down onto the edge of his old bed, floating deeper into dreams of what might lie ahead for him, Peter felt human already.

Bonnie tiptoed down the long staircase, easing her muddy sneakers onto the steps so slowly and carefully. The beast had hearing more sensitive than that of a regular person. One false step could bring him running. She could hear him in his room, making a strange sound in the back of his throat. Good. It would help cover up any stray squeak or bump. But what was it he was doing in there? The noise got louder as Bonnie approached the second-floor landing. It was a rough but strangely lilting sound, almost melodic—a song, yes, that's what it was! The beast was in his room, singing away!

Bonnie felt a tickle of bittersweet warmth for the beast. Now that she was getting away from him, she could admit it. What a peculiar and sad creature he was. At once a spoiled, bossy child and a worldly man with an appetite for adventure that was as big as hers. A powerful creature, but a powerfully lonely one. And yet here he was singing. The beast was singing out loud.

Bonnie recognized the swell of guilt in her. She knew why he was so happy that night. *It's because he thinks you're his friend. Because he has a special guest to make his days less lonely now.* What if some evil spirit had come and turned her into a horrible beast, someone who could never be part of the world again? Would she so easily give up the only human company she had?

She paused on the stairwell landing. She wished she could go down the hall and knock on the beast's door. Say a proper and civilized goodbye. Promise to come back and lunch with him in some exotic part of the world. Maybe even shake his big paw. But she knew what would happen if she did. He would show his sharp teeth, let out a roar, and throw her back upstairs with no way to get out.

She held back a sigh and continued to creep down the stairs. She could see into the living room from here, the edge of an antique chair, the ripped but once-luxurious rug, the spare, polished pedestal on which sat the vase with the single rose. Who would know by looking at the room now that it was a gateway to a world of different places?

Bonnie would miss the magic of this house. She knew she would long for it once the same old routine of Land's End set in again. But soon she would be home hugging her father tightly. Soon she would sleep in her own modest, comfortable room again. Soon she would be free. And the beast wasn't going to deny her that any longer.

She put her hand on the cold, shiny brass doorknob and turned it slowly. She felt her muscles jerk tensely as the catch tumbled open with a loud, metallic click. She cast a fearful glance up the stairs, then pulled the door open fast and carelessly and raced out into the night.

The fresh, sweet air hit her face, giving her a burst of energy. Her long legs stretched out as she ran. Her heart beat wildly. She wasn't scot-free yet. But the inky sky over her head was limitless, the hazy moon cast just enough light to illuminate the way, and the walls of the Lair got farther away with every step she took.

"Grrr!" The beast's growl came out of thin air.

"Oh, no!" Bonnie screamed as he leaped into

her path, springing a surprise attack as only a stealthy animal could do.

He flung her to the ground with one push of his paws. Bonnie was too stunned to move. "You lied to me!" he roared. "I trusted you! You promised!"

Bonnie tried to recover her breath. "And what's a promise to someone who takes prisoners without a second thought?"

"How would you know what it's like to be trapped in the body of a wild animal? How would you know how many second thoughts I might have had?" the beast roared back. As Bonnie struggled to get back on her feet, he threw his weight at her and knocked her down again.

"Thoughts? What savage beast has thoughts?" Bonnie shrieked. "Thoughts or feelings? You may have fooled me once or twice, but you're not even close to human!"

The beast snarled and gnashed his teeth. Bonnie wondered how she could have ever paused for a second as she fled the house. In the moonlight, as the beast howled and frothed at the mouth, she could see his true nature. "Why, I'll bet you were never human for a day of your life!" she went on furiously. "I'll bet that whole story about the enchantress was an even bigger lie than the one I told you!"

The beast's roar shook the very leaves on the trees. "Is that what you really think? That I don't have any human thoughts or feelings? Didn't you see how I felt about you? I'm less of a beast than a total fool, thinking you might see through my ugliness to the person inside!"

"Person, ha!" Bonnie shot back as she slowly rose again. This time the beast didn't try to keep her down. "Even if I did believe your wild story, that enchantress only made you look the way you really are."

"Then go!" the beast roared. "And never tease me with promises of friendship again. If this is a human bond, than you can take it with you." He pulled back into a tightly wound crouch. "I thought maybe I'd found the girl of my dreams, but I see my dreams are better left unfulfilled. Why did I ever let myself hope? Go back to your nothing town and your nothing life, pretty Bonnie. Go."

This time Bonnie didn't hesitate. This time there was no smidgeon of remorse. She ran as fast as she could, and she didn't look back.

Down the mountain she went, crashing through the brush and sliding on loose rubble, anger coursing through her body.

"Human inside. Right," she muttered. She didn't care about the low branches slashing at her or the raw, breathless feeling in her throat. The beast had done her a favor just now. There wasn't any part of her that felt the least bit sorry anymore for leaving him all alone. Let him howl himself sick up there with all his fancy trickery and money to burn. Let him cry by himself over the long-ago times when he hadn't been a—

Beast! The eyes glimmered evilly, two diamond-bright points in the darkness ahead. Bonnie's anger surged. He'd changed his mind. He'd come after her once again.

"No! I won't let you get me," she shouted, not slowing down.

She heard a low, sharp snarling. There was something different about the sound. She glanced back over her shoulder. There was something not quite familiar about those eyes. . . .

Suddenly she saw two more glowing pairs, and another pair and another. "Help me!" she whispered, her anger turning to the deepest fear.

The snarling escalated, the noise of many beasts in vicious concert. She stopped running, frozen with terror. Her eyes picked out the sleek silver forms. *The wolf pack,* Bonnie thought, her muscles going weak. *The same one that attacked Dad.*

"No!" Her scream of terror pierced the night. And then they were moving toward her as one.

It was as if it were happening in slow motion. The deadly, graceful stride of the wolves coming at her; the sound from their throats like a chorus of eerie, wailing foghorns, signaling danger; the flashing teeth.

"Help! Stop!" Bonnie cried, holding her hands up in front of her face. She was never going to make it off this mountain alive. She didn't even feel the first slash. She just surrendered to the ground, her body numb beneath her lethal attackers.

So this was where it ended. On the forest floor with no chance of being saved. It was almost as if it were happening to someone else, and Bonnie was outside of it, floating above the terrifying scene and watching detachedly. As if she were already gone from this world.

But suddenly the wolves abandoned her, leaving her gasping in the dirt almost before they'd touched her. Bonnie turned her head to see them bounding toward a new target: a huge, growling creature, wildly plunging into their midst almost as if to draw their attack.

Bonnie pushed herself up on her feet. Oh, no, it was the beast!

"Run, Bonnie, run!" he cried as the wolves surrounded him. Then he was snarling and his own teeth were flashing. The whole picture was just a violent blur.

But Bonnie couldn't budge. The beast had come to save her. The beast. Not some perfect fairy-tale hero. And he was going to die trying. For her. No! She couldn't let them kill the beast. But what could she possibly do? She stood there helplessly, the acrid smell of the fight burning her nostrils and chilling her blood.

But then she saw one of the wolves go down. And then another. Could he bring down the entire wolf pack? A beast who couldn't even watch them kill a bull? *Oh, beast!* Bonnie thought, willing him to stay strong and invincible.

His cries were eerie—part animal, part human, and separate from the vicious sounds of the wolves. Bonnie could pick them out even though the furry bodies were never still long enough for her to get a clear view of the battle. The battle to the death.

Bonnie was not aware of breathing until the last animal had fallen to the dark earth. Then she crept forward cautiously, her heart in her throat. "Beast?" she whispered in the sudden still of the night. *Let him be alive!* she prayed.

The beast let out a groan of pain. At least he hadn't been killed! Bonnie let out a sigh of relief as she sank down next to him. Out of the corner of her eye Bonnie saw a wolf limping away from them. Another whimpered nearby. Several lay where they were, not moving. But the beast was hurt, too, and badly. Patches of his fur had been torn right off, and blood oozed from jagged wounds.

"Look what they've done to you," Bonnie cried.

He turned his swollen eyes to her. "And you, Bonnie? Tell me that you're okay," he whispered hoarsely. "Your arm—you're bleeding."

Bonnie hadn't felt the deep scratch on her left forearm until now. Blood beaded up in a dark red line, and she became aware of a throbbing pain. But it was nothing compared to what could have been. And nothing compared to the sorry state of the beast. Yet here he was, concerned about *her*. Was this the same creature who, only a short time back, had dragged her through his front door with his teeth?

"I'm fine," Bonnie said. "I mean, I'm lucky just to be alive. But you . . ."

"I'm here, too. Maybe a little worse for wear." The beast managed a feeble laugh.

"Oh, but look at your paw," Bonnie cried, noticing for the first time the bloody pulp at the end of one of his hind legs.

The beast moaned as he curled the leg in to inspect it. "One of them got a whole meal out of it," he agreed. "But it'll heal sooner or later. I guess I'll be doing a lot of sitting at my table at Café l'Illusion for a while, watching the world go by. A beast could do a lot worse, you know."

But the beast's cyber-jaunts suddenly seemed so lonely to Bonnie. So clearly a substitute for the life he couldn't live. She felt an unshed tear well up in her eye. "Well, at least let me help you get back to the Lai—your house."

"No," the beast said, without any anger. "I set you free, and that's not going to change."

"And I want to go home to my father, to where I belong," Bonnie said. "That's not going to change, either. But let me help you home and make sure you're okay. I can start back tomorrow. It'll be so much easier when it's light out, anyway."

"Thank you, Bonnie. You don't know how much it means to me. But only if you're really sure . . ."

Bonnie gave a decisive nod. Next to them, one

of the wolves stirred and let loose a halfhearted snarl.

"Well, then, we'd better get moving now," the beast said. "Before this pack regroups." The beast lumbered up to stand on three paws, the fourth one dangling uselessly a few inches above the ground.

Bonnie grimaced. "I'm so sorry, beast."

"Sorry? That the wolves didn't make a meal of *you?*"

"You saved my life, even though I turned my back on you."

"And you've agreed to be a real, true guest in my house this evening, even though I know it's the last thing you thought you wanted to do. You know, I've never had a real guest before." The beast let out a soft groan of pain as he took a limping step back in the direction of the Lair. "You know the expression 'I'd give my right arm for this'?"

"It's your left leg, and we're going to have it bandaged up in no time," Bonnie assured him.

Thirteen

It was a night of firsts. First real guest. First time since the fateful transformation that the beast had strolled along the cliffside path past the boundaries of his own private turf. First time he'd been happy—really happy—in, well, too many years even to say.

"Where to?" he'd asked after Bonnie had helped Rita minister to his wounds. Oh, Bonnie's touch, so light and tentative, yet—yes—tender. How concerned she'd been about whether she was hurting him as she'd wrapped the gauze bandage around his paw. As if her genuine caring wasn't worth any pain he might endure. "A trip to see the northern lights? A concert of Indian music?" he'd suggested.

But Bonnie, her scratched arm cleaned and bandaged, had shaken her head. Her glossy, spun-toffee hair swirled around her shoulders.

"How about just a walk outside? It's such a mild night. I want to hear the ocean—and know that it's real. Smell the wild beach plums, feel the wind. What's your favorite place to walk around here?"

The beast had been startled at her simple question. He rarely left the walls of his house anymore, except in the safety of his computer-generated travels. He remembered the gruesome incident, so many years ago, when he'd found himself in the woods, lunging at a small cotton-tail bunny, almost as if he had no control over what he was doing. Since then he'd mostly stayed inside or kept to the confines of his own property.

"Well, I think once upon a time there was a path that ran along the length of the cliff," he'd answered. He had a vague memory of walking there with his mother, but it had been so many, many years ago that it was far less real than the false reality of a place like the Café l'Illusion.

But now he was back on the path again, the ocean sparkling below him and Bonnie in the soft, hazy moonlight. The way was overgrown, but the long grasses tickled his fur pleasantly as he walked—or, more accurately, hobbled, his bandaged paw throbbing painfully.

But there was a sense of liberation as he followed the twisting and turning path, leaving his house behind him and out of view. With the sky and sea his only boundaries, he couldn't ignore the simple truth that he too was a prisoner in that fancy, everything-money-could-buy home. And this was another first: He finally had at least a slight inkling of what Bonnie had been longing for when she cried for freedom in her glass tower.

"I never should have kept you with me—not a single night," he said to her now. A rough wave crashed against the bottom of the cliff. "But I couldn't understand what you must have been feeling. It's been such a long time since I remembered what human emotions were like. It was so long ago for me. . . . But that's no excuse, is it?"

Bonnie was looking at him curiously. She was so beautiful, her face awash with silvery moonlight. "Beast, I was too afraid to ask before. Or maybe I didn't care enough. But what you told me about the enchantress—about how you acted so beastly and became a . . . beast. After, um . . . well, after this thing was done to you, the enchantress just disappeared, and that was the end? I mean, there's nothing you can do to make it up? No way you can get changed back from—from—"

"From this grotesque thing that I've become?" The beast stifled the roar that swelled in his throat.

"I didn't mean it that way," Bonnie said.

The beast thought of the pink rose, still perfect, but not for long. Should he tell Bonnie what the enchantress had told him that night? That there *was* a way to become human again? Should he beg for Bonnie's love and her power to restore him to manhood? Cry that his beastly selfishness with her was really desperation?

No, he couldn't. She would only pity him, and that wasn't love. The beast lifted his massive shoulders in a shrug. "Is it so—so awful, being here with a beast?"

Bonnie was silent for a moment. Then she shook her head. "No. No, it's not." She sounded surprised at herself. "Until tonight my answer would have been different. But tonight I'm walking under the stars with my friend—not with a beast."

The beast felt the moistness in his eyes. And then the slow trickle of it down his face. *Oh, my goodness, tears!* Tears that had dried up all those years ago. Tears he didn't even know this beast's body could shed. "That doesn't mean you'll stay here, does it?" he asked. He didn't dare to hope.

The moonlight caught the glitter of her own moist eyes. She shook her head. "I miss my father so much," she said. "He must be so terribly, terribly worried about me."

The beast nodded. "When he was here, all he could think about was you. I didn't know two people could care so much about each other," he said. At least he hadn't known it before he'd met Bonnie. Now . . . well, now he knew he loved Bonnie as much as a beast could love anyone. Her fight and her intelligent sensitivity. Her spirit of adventure. Her love of nature and the sea. And yes, her beautiful, beautiful face and figure, too. And he knew there was nothing more important than making her happy. Nothing. Including his own humanity.

"Go to your father, Bonnie," he said. "Go home to him. Arno will drive you there in the morning."

Bonnie's reply was to reach out and touch him gently on the arm. A soft, gentle pet of his fur for just the briefest moment. He knew that meant she would be leaving the next day. And he knew for certain he loved her, because his heart was breaking.

They had a bon voyage breakfast in Cabo de Aguazul, a pink beach with turquoise water as smooth as a lake. Their table sat right in the sugar-fine sand, and Bonnie dug her feet through the warm top layer into the coolness underneath.

They were alone. The meal had already been spread on the table when they'd arrived—sweet fried bananas, creamy coffee, and garlicky eggs with a crunchy cucumber-peanut relish. The table was set with a white linen cloth, the pink rose in a conch-shell vase in the center. There was no sign of the beast's Arno, even in tropical disguise, nor any cyber-beachers politely oblivious to the beast's condition.

But even without those reminders that this paradise was only electronic magic, and even with the spectacular scenery and exotic food, Bonnie was too far removed to let herself truly believe in any of this. Far more real was the quiet sadness of the beast, his face swollen and bruised from his battle with the wolves, the look in his eyes more human than animal.

His marvelous machine was supposed to make him part of the world, to let him drink in the sights and sounds that would otherwise be lost to him. But it only took him farther away from reality, Bonnie thought. It drew him deeper and deeper into his fantasy world. A world that wasn't real. A world in which he was alone. It could only make him lonelier and more solitary.

Bonnie took a sip of her coffee. It was delicious, and so was the rest of the meal, but she took little pleasure in it and finally pushed her plate away. "I promise I'll visit you," she told the beast. "I'll come back, and we'll explore the world together."

"My door is always open to you, Bonnie," the beast said.

They sat without saying anything more for a while. The water lapped against the pink shore. What if it could be real? Bonnie found herself wishing. What if she and the beast could actually travel the world outside the Lair? Oh, but traveling the globe with a beast for a companion—it was too absurd even to consider.

"Well, let's not put it off any longer," the beast finally said. And with that the tropical beach simply melted away. Bonnie found herself sitting on the beast's couch in bare feet, not even a single grain of sand between her toes.

Her dirty sneakers were on the floor next to her. Reluctantly she slipped them on and stood up. She took a final look around the room. The rose was back on its pedestal. She went over and took a fragrant smell. "Always at the peak of its bloom," she mused. "It's so beautiful. Do you have someone supply them fresh each day?"

The beast went over and eased the flower from its vase, using both awkward paws to do it.

"Would you believe me if I told you it was the same flower day after day? Month after month? That it has been fresh and perfect for a long, long time?"

"You've told me some really strange things," Bonnie replied. "A perfect flower . . . well, maybe it's not any more impossible than a boy turned into a beast." *The Lair is such a dizzying place,* she thought. Where what seemed real wasn't, and where the unreal was real.

The beast held the flower out to her now. "Please take it as a gift—a reminder of our time together. I'm afraid it won't be perfect for too much longer, but of everything I own, it's my most special possession."

Bonnie took the rose, careful not to prick her finger on a thorn. "Thank you, beast. I'll treasure it for as long as it blooms. But there's something else I want you to give me."

"The blue dress I bought you in Italy. You'll find it in the limo in a bag on the backseat. The red one you liked more is in there, too. I'm sorry I was such a beast about that. It really looked beautiful on you, too."

Bonnie felt a wave of tenderness for him. "Thank you. I'll be happy to take the dresses home. But that's not what I was thinking about, actually. There's something else."

"Anything. Anything at all."

A little shyly, Bonnie asked the question she'd been wondering about since the previous night. "What was your name when you were a boy? What is your name, beast? You do have a name, don't you?"

The beast nodded. "You want my name as a going-away gift? I'd be happy to tell you. It's Peter. Peter Crowley. Pleased to meet you," he added sadly.

"Peter," she repeated, wishing she could imagine what he'd looked like then. And as his name rolled off her tongue, his expression brightened into a smile. "Peter, you're the most human beast I could ever imagine," Bonnie said sincerely. Holding the rose carefully, she reached up and circled her arms around his huge body in a hug. His fur was so soft—she'd been surprised by its silkiness when she'd touched him on their walk the night before. As she clung to him she had a silly, frustrating instant of wishing he were still a boy—or, rather, a man, who could take her in his arms and sweep her off her feet.

"Good-bye," she said, releasing him with a sigh. "Good-bye, beast. Good-bye, Peter."

"Go, Bonnie, before I can't let you," he said.

He ushered her toward the front door and opened it.

Out in front of the house, Arno honked the horn of a vintage limo. Bonnie put the rose to her face. "I'll think of you," she said. "And I'll be back soon."

She stepped out of the Lair and walked to the car. Freedom had a distinctly bittersweet taste that morning.

Fourteen

Gary was in the mood for a fight. He and Pat and Mark bounced up the road in his truck, and each time the tires hit hard against a pit or a crack, he let the rough bump fuel his aggression like a flint being struck. This time he wasn't going to stop at the gates to the Lair. This time he was going in, even if he had to break the door down. Bats and clubs clattered in the rear of the truck. No child's stones and bottles on this trip. And Gary had a steel surprise packed in his sock, hard and cold and excitingly lethal against his ankle.

He pressed his foot down on the accelerator and heard the satisfying scream of rubber as he raced ahead too fast on the country road.

"Grrr. One big, strong man's gonna get him some woman," Pat said, laughing like a moronic hyena.

"Yeah, he's gonna show that precious thing that a Land's End guy is more than good enough for her," Mark chimed in.

Gary grinned. "You bet I am. Me and you and a few well-placed blows to that monster's head. But don't get too hasty, now, do you read me? She's gotta beg me to save her first. Beg like a dog."

"Arf, arf. Way to go," cackled Pat. "We've gotta put those gals in their place, you know? Whoever let 'em out of the kitchen to begin with? Me, I'm getting me a woman who'll have a steak dinner on the table when I come home."

Gary didn't bother to tell Pat that a Neanderthal like him would be lucky to get any woman at all. He was feeling too good. Soon these two goons would be riding back home to Land's End in the bed of the truck, and Bonnie would be up here next to him, gazing at him adoringly. Yeah, he was going to have the most beautiful girlfriend in Land's End. And she was going to be grateful to him, too.

Gary squealed around a sharp turn. A blaring horn split the air a second before he saw the shiny black limo. He jerked the steering wheel, pulling the car away from the middle of the road. What was that fat hog of a rich person's car doing around here, anyway? The summer season must be starting already.

"Out of my way," Gary said as he barreled by the long car. "Some of us have some hunting to do. And when we're through, we're going to be bringing back a prize." Very, very soon he was going to have the desirable but elusive Bonnie Oliviera eating out of his hand.

"Dad, Dad!" Bonnie burst into the house and raced from room to room. The simple, clean-lined, familiar furnishings, the warm redwood floors and the braided living room rug, the cozy but gracious look of the place—she was home! Bonnie was home!

"Bonnie! *Querida!* My little girl!" Her father emerged from the kitchen, a broken clock in one hand, a screwdriver in the other, as if her absence had stopped time for him. He let everything clatter to the floor and threw his arms around her, hugging her tightly. "My special girl. Bonnie. I was so afraid I'd lost you to that beast."

Bonnie hugged her father hard, the pink rose still clutched in one hand. It was so good to see him and hear his voice again, so good to be back in the place she belonged. Okay, so maybe the house did seem rather small and ordinary after the Lair. Maybe there weren't any exotic surprises hidden in the walls. But she was home! Finally. She'd thought it might never happen.

"I wondered when I'd see you, too. Oh, Daddy, I thought about you every second," she said. "I was so worried about you. I missed you so incredibly much."

"Well, I'm just fine, now that you're here. It's so wonderful to have you home. Oh, but are you okay? Did that beast hurt you? Bonnie, what's this bandage on your arm? He *did* hurt you. I'll kill him. I'll kill the beast!"

Bonnie felt a beat of alarm. "No, you don't understand. It wasn't the beast. He didn't hurt me. Not a bit." She released herself from her father's hug. "This bandage, well . . . Oh, there's so much to tell you, but the most important thing is that I'm here."

"Thank goodness," her father added. "Thank goodness for that Belsky boy."

"Excuse me?" Bonnie felt a jolt of confusion.

"That boy from your school. Chief Belsky's nephew—Gary."

Bonnie tensed up. "Gary Belsky? Daddy, what does Gary have to do with my being home again?" Hadn't it been bad enough to have the first car they'd passed in Land's End be Gary's road hog of a truck? Gary was the last person in town she ever wanted to see again. At least he hadn't able to see her through the limo's dark windows. But apparently he wasn't out of the picture yet.

A startled look passed across her father's face. "He went up there to get you. To rescue you. He told me he was going this morning with two of his friends."

"Oh, no." It was starting to make sense. That was why Gary had been barreling up the road in such a hurry. Bonnie's chest felt tight. What would Gary do to the beast when he got there?

"We've got to go after them right away," Bonnie said. She was already heading back out the door.

"Wait!" Her father ran after her. "You can't go. I just got you back. Those boys—they can take care of themselves. They didn't go up there empty-handed, I'm sure."

"That's what I'm afraid of," Bonnie said. "Oh, wait. You'll have to give me the keys to your truck."

Her father put a firm hand on her arm. "You are *not* going up there again. And what exactly are you afraid of?"

"Daddy, you don't understand. The beast has

changed. I'm here because he sent me home to you. And now those—those *real* beasts are going up there to hurt him."

"And what do you think you can do about it? Bonnie, sweetie, don't you think the beast can defend himself quite well all on his own? He managed to destroy his own living room in about two minutes flat, if I remember correctly."

But Bonnie was remembering instead the brave way the beast had fought the wolf pack. Then she recalled his bloody, useless paw—that plus the fact that no beast, no matter how strong or clever, was a match for the deadliness of the human weapons Gary might have.

"You have to trust me, Daddy. The beast needs our help. And he deserves it. Daddy, he saved my life as well as yours. Oh, there's no time to talk about it now, but you've got to believe me. You'll see for yourself. Or maybe you won't, but I'm going up there whether you want me to or not."

Her father looked grim, but he nodded. "Well, if you're going up there, I am, too. No chance you're going alone." He pulled the truck keys out of his pants pocket with a jangle. "I only hope you know what you're doing."

Bonnie brought the pink flower to her nose

and inhaled the sweet perfume. "I do," she said firmly. "But we have to hurry." At the rate Gary had been driving, it might already be too late. The beast had saved her from the jaws of the wolves. Would she be able to save him now?

Fifteen

The beast had that funny, hungry feeling in his stomach again. But no, it wasn't hunger this time. He looked out the oval tower window down toward the port of Land's End. It was the same awful sensation he'd tried to shut out after his parents' accident. The same feeling he used to swallow with a savage roar. But now he was starting to understand the feeling, and he was sure a roar could only chase it deeper down inside of himself. It was fear and loneliness that were overtaking him.

"Bonnie." He mouthed her name.

Would she be true to her word and visit him in this vast house from time to time? Or had he lost her forever when the limo pulled away? The beast wondered what she was doing right at that moment. Perhaps she was heading for the harbor and the boat she'd described in such loving detail. Was she climbing over the rail onto the *Bonita II,* with its crazy gadgets and inventions? Or was she celebrating her homecoming in the coffee shop where her father started his day? At that very second, whatever she was doing in Land's End seemed infinitely more appealing than the biggest adventure in the farthest reaches of the globe could ever be.

The beast put a paw—one of his good ones—on the back of the chair by the curved bank of windows. Bonnie had sat here. But she probably never would aga—

Boom, boom, boom!

The banging on the door downstairs startled the beast out of his sad musings. A spark of hope flared in him. Had she come back? Had Bonnie changed her mind?

But even as he was bounding down the steps on three paws, he heard Rita's frightened voice. "Who are you? What do you want?"

The beast reached the bottom landing in a few more leaps. A trio of angry-looking young men were pushing their way past Rita into the house. One of them wielded a baseball bat. Another dragged a massive, deadly-looking steel chain.

"Where is he?" he heard one of them demand.

But when they spotted him, they went slack

with fear. The beast let out his fiercest roar. His huge chest swelled even bigger at the terror that was written across their faces. Two of them were frozen to the spot.

But the third seemed to swallow his fear and take a tentative step toward the beast. On instinct, the beast went into a crouch. One false move from this guy and he would pounce. His black talons emerged knifelike from the soft pads of all but the wounded paw. He pulled his lips back in a grimace, flashing sharp teeth.

The young man flinched, but he held his ground. "Where are you keeping her?" he demanded menacingly.

The beast didn't have to ask who. In an instant all the fight went out of him. He let out a plaintive howl as he looked at the specimen in front of him: handsome, blond, strapping, not to mention tough enough to confront a savage animal. How could the beast imagine for a second that Bonnie would come back to him, a hideous creature who wasn't anything close to a man?

"She went back home," the beast said resignedly. "You just missed her on her way to town."

The young man gave a derisive laugh. "You'll excuse me if I don't believe you, you disgusting freak of nature."

Rita stepped up to the beast's side. "It's true," she said. "The young lady—Bonnie—she left just a little while ago. Now go. We don't want any trouble here."

"Shut up, you old hag! You've gotta be some kind of witch to live with a monster like this." The young man's disgust twisted his chiseled features into something ugly.

The beast gave a low growl. "I forbid you to talk that way. Now go. You heard what the lady said."

"And you heard what I said. I want to know where Bonnie is. I'm here to get her and I'm not leaving until I have her."

"I'm telling you the truth. She isn't here."

He turned to his sidekicks. "Get a load of the truthful beast. Do we believe him? Huh? Say something, big men. Pat, do we believe him?"

The stringy-haired one called Pat managed a shake of his head.

"Mark, do we believe him?"

"Gary, m-maybe we should just get out of here, you know?" Mark's voice quivered.

Gary. Where have I heard that name before? the beast wondered.

"There are plenty of other pretty girls in Land's End," Mark went on fearfully.

"You make me sick, Mark," Gary said. "Watch a real man in action and learn something."

The beast was starting to feel sick himself. How could Bonnie like this brute? Sensitive, smart Bonnie. Oh, if only the beast had a man's face and body to give her.

Gary made a move toward the beast. The beast gave a warning growl. "I don't want to have to do it, but I can rip you apart before you even know what's happening." He was on his guard, his muscles tensed to go into action.

Suddenly Gary dropped down and reached toward one ankle. There was a flash of silver and a cold, loud click. He and the beast sprang at the same moment.

"Take that," Gary said. The beast felt a hot, searing pain rip through his soft underbelly. The switchblade cut a deep tear in his flesh.

"No!" Rita's cry met the beast's own.

The beast crumpled to the floor, aware of the warm, sticky blood oozing out of him far too quickly. He struggled to get back on his feet, but his body wouldn't obey his will. *Get up. Fight,* the beast in him insisted.

But what difference does it make, anyway? he thought. Bonnie had left, and she wasn't coming back. Why pretend it was any other way? And the beast—he would be trapped in this ogre's shell forever. Condemned, alone. He gave up, and his muscles went weak and limp. He put his head down on the floor in defeat. If only he could see her sweet, round face one more time. Then he could perish in peace.

"Beast! Peter, what has he done?" Bonnie's voice reached his ears, as if his final wish had come true. He had to be imagining it. This wasn't real. But he snapped his head up, and there she was.

"Bonnie?"

Her beautiful blue eyes were big with fear. "Peter, you're bleeding." She rushed toward him and dropped down by his side. "What did you do?" she roared at Gary. "You monster. You . . . thing!" The beast could feel her hand, resting on his back, tremble with rage. Rage at his attackers, but such wondrously sweet concern for him.

"You came back!" he said in amazement. "You're here." He felt a bit of strength flowing back into him. She hadn't abandoned him after all.

"I'm right beside you," she said. "And my father is here, too." Tony Oliviera stood in the doorway. "But we have to get you some medical attention right away. Rita, is there someone we can call? Daddy, maybe you should go for a doctor!"

"You mean a veterinarian," Gary snorted. "Bonnie, I actually think you have feelings for this revolting animal."

The beast felt Bonnie's arm muscles tighten. He saw her look up at Gary. She couldn't miss the switchblade, wet with the beast's own blood.

"What would you know of feelings?" Bonnie spat at him.

The beast felt a surge of wonder through his pain. He felt light yet full of pleasure at the same time, and as wonderfully dizzy as if he had been running circles in a meadow of brilliant, sweet wildflowers. He felt . . . joy. That was what this sensation was. Bonnie had feelings for him. And clearly not for handsome, brutish Gary.

Gary's face turned beet red with rage. The beast could feel the danger in him. He wore the scent and attitude of impending violence. "You care about a beast, an animal, an ogre?" he thundered. "When I get finished with him, it'll be too late to call anyone."

"I'm safe," Bonnie said with equal fury. "You came to rescue me, and I don't need rescuing. Go on, Gary. You've done your damage. Get out of here. Right now."

"This is the thanks I get!" Gary yelled. "Open your eyes, Bonnie. Look at what he is. He's a beast. A monster. A mutation. A menace to society. He locked you up here. What's to say he won't be kidnapping someone else's daughter next?" He took a step toward the beast, his knife held out. "Mark, Pat, we have a duty to do here. For our town. For the safety of the children of Land's End. Get moving, guys. Do you want me to tell everyone how you just stood there and shivered like two little mama's boys?"

"Gary, no! He's hurt badly enough," Bonnie cried out.

"Out of my way," Gary sneered in reply. He lunged at her and gave her a hard shove, sending her reeling backward.

With his acute side vision, the beast saw Bonnie's father rush over to her. At the same second, Gary made his move toward the beast, leading with the tip of his knife. The beast felt a swell of strength. He didn't want to lie down and give up anymore. Bonnie cared about him. She was his friend. A few minutes before, it hadn't mattered to him if he lived or died. In the space of a heartbeat, all that had changed.

The beast pounced, his talons sinking into Gary's soft flesh.

"Yeow!" Gary cried out in pain.

The beast bared his teeth, but suddenly something solid came down with a thud on his head. He felt himself rolling off Gary and caught a glimpse of one of Gary's sidekicks holding a baseball bat and getting ready to strike again. The beast lunged, dimly aware of the pain in his bad paw and the sharp, warm burning where his body had been cut. He rammed his body into Gary's friend's stomach and knocked the wind right out of him.

"Oof!" He heard the satisfying sound as the friend went down and the bat clattered out of his hand.

But here was Gary and the glinting, bloody knife again. And the other friend, equipped with a sinister-looking, heavy chain that he whirled around like a lasso. The beast deftly jumped away from the chain, though he felt a crippling pain shoot through his stomach again.

As he paused for a split second to let the pain ebb, he was caught with another club of the baseball bat on his back from behind. And before he could take a breath, all three of his attackers were on top of him.

"Kill him!" one of the boys yelled.

The beast lashed out, his teeth piercing bare, hairless skin, his tongue tasting blood. A wild scream went up. He scratched, he tore skin. He snarled and bit.

But the heavy chain smashed into his head, and his vision was blurred by his own blood. He raked his nails in midair, his tender belly exposed and vulnerable. He wasn't quick enough to roll over to protect himself. Above his left breast came another searing tear of the knife. His heart!

He yowled in pain. The cut had pierced him in the worst place of all. He willed his muscles to keep fighting, but he felt himself collapsing onto the floor.

"Peter! No!" he heard Bonnie yelling. Her voice sounded as if it were coming from far away. He couldn't move. Not even a limb. The grinning, malicious faces of his attackers loomed over him.

And then everything in his vision wavered and blurred. The whole room seemed to be receding, vanishing into a long tunnel, at the end of which was a bright light. This was no cyber-dream, no computerized journey. He felt himself drawn toward the light. He wanted to bathe in its warmth and soothing energy. His body was light. He was floating, floating down the tunnel toward—

"No! No! You can't die, Peter. Don't die!" Bonnie's voice followed him down the tunnel and caught him fast. He felt the weight returning to his body. The weight, but also the throbbing, almost unbearable pain. He wanted the light, he wanted the release. But he also wanted Bonnie. He wanted her hand on him as his life ebbed away. . . .

Gary and company watched him with evil satisfaction. "End of problem," Gary said coolly, as if he'd squashed a bug.

"Oh, no! Don't let it be true," Bonnie cried.

The beast felt himself getting pulled closer to the flood of light. "If they're what it means to be human, then I might as well die," he whispered, using every last ounce of remaining strength to get the words out. "They're nothing more than cruel and wild animals."

And then he remembered why he knew Gary's name. He was the one Bonnie had told him about. The guy she knew who acted like an awful beast. No, he didn't want to be anything like that. Better to get swallowed up in the dazzling light that was beckoning to him. "But at least I got to see you once more, Bonnie. That's all I really wanted."

"And what about what I want?" Bonnie

asked. "What about me?" Her words brought him crashing back down to earth. "I don't want you to die, Peter. I love you."

The words he'd never, ever expected to hear echoed down his tunnel of light. *She loves me.* He was filled with wonder and joy. *Bonnie loves the beast. Bonnie loves Peter. She loves me.*

Her declaration caught him and held him fast. He would go down the tunnel one day. He would bathe in the light. But not now. He turned away from it, and the light faded. The living room came back into focus. Tears streamed down Bonnie's beautiful face.

"Don't cry," he wanted to tell her. "I won't leave you." But something very, very strange was happening in his limbs, his body, his muscles, and his nerves. His mouth was twisting uncontrollably, and he couldn't form the words. He felt a kind of yawning ache spreading through his body. Was this what dying was like? Was he going to slip away from Bonnie after all, no matter what he decided?

The beast felt himself overcome by some kind of transformation. And there wasn't a thing he could do to stop it from happening.

Bonnie stared aghast at the blood that drenched the beast's shirt and pants, pooling around him on the polished wood floor. His eyes were glazed and had a faraway look. "Don't die. I love you," she repeated. And as she said it she knew it was true. They had so many new places to visit and so many adventures to live. So much to discover together, so much to share.

But Gary's knife had dealt a blow to the heart. Bonnie dropped down and took the beast's paw. It was weak, limp, and—

"Oh, no!" Bonnie cried out as she dropped it in shock. His paw was lengthening, narrowing, the fur fading, the black talonlike nails shrinking. "What's going on?"

And then she saw that his body was changing, the features of his face shifting . . . His whole body was undergoing some kind of metamorphosis!

"Look!" Gary let out a cry of alarm—or was it one of Gary's friends? Bonnie didn't take her eyes off the beast for a second to see who'd uttered the cry. *The beast. Oh, my beast. Peter. Yes—that's it! Peter!*

Bonnie gasped as she realized what was happening. The beast was turning back into a boy! Or, rather, a man. A tall, handsome man with strong, full features and thick, wavy hair just as golden as his fur. His eyes were dark blue, the same blue they'd been all along, and when she looked into them, Bonnie could see the most human of souls.

And then she saw another thing, too. Beneath the ripped shirt and pants that now swam enormously on his lean body, his wounds were starting to close up. Even the blood on the floor was simply disappearing. Color flowed to his cheeks and face. His gaze grew clear as it held hers.

He lifted up a strong, slender hand, and the oversized bandages from his wounded paw fell away. He brought his hand to his face and traced its new contours. Bonnie watched the growing realization in his eyes—and then the unbounded joy.

"Bonnie, I love you, too," he whispered in amazement. His voice was more refined, yet somehow the same.

Bonnie reached out and touched the hand he held to his face. She felt an electric thrill as their fingers intertwined, learning together the new feel of his full lips, his cheekbones, the arch of his eyebrows, the strong brow.

"It's true, isn't it?" he said, laughing as tears of happiness slipped from his eyes. "I'm a boy . . . a man, and I'm with you? I haven't died and gone to heaven after all?"

He gathered her in his arms. She held him in a fierce hug. "If you have, so have I," she answered.

But it wasn't heaven, and it wasn't a dream. She could see her father and Rita standing right there, looking on in happy amazement. Gary, Pat, and Mark were edging toward the door. "Shouldn't we stop them?" Bonnie whispered.

Peter held her close. "I'm not taking any more prisoners," he said. "Let them go and never come back. And now tell me what you told me before."

"That I love you?" Bonnie whispered. "I love you, Peter. I love you, my beast."

And then her lips found his in the sweetest, most tender, wildest kiss. . . .

Epilogue

Tony Oliviera was sitting in the little Portuguese cyber-bar with the beautiful wall tiles, having a strong, creamy coffee.

Across the small, square pitted wooden table from him, Rita was sipping one, too. "Mmm. Is the coffee this good in the real Bar Passa-tempo?"

Bonnie's father took a sip of his foamy drink. He laughed and shrugged. "To tell you the truth, I'd barely started drinking coffee before I left my country. It tastes like this in my memory, but who knows?" He took another sip. "It was so long ago. More like a dream than anything I can remember clearly."

"And aren't you curious?" Rita asked. "Don't you want to know what the real Bar Passatempo is like now?"

Tony was thoughtful. "Well, yes. And no.

You know, the bea—I mean, Peter created this bar from everything I told him. From all the romantic ideas I have in my head about my hometown and the places I spent time in as a boy. But maybe the tiles on the walls of the real Bar Passatempo aren't nearly so colorful and jewel-like. Maybe the place isn't so dark and cozy. Maybe Arno's computerized brew is better than the real thing."

"You mean you don't want to find out that this place exists only in your memory?" Rita said.

"You think that's silly."

"No. No, not at all," Rita assured him. Her soft, gently lined face was sympathetic. "Until Bonnie set Peter free—and Arno and I and the rest of us were set free with him—I felt the same way about the world outside these walls. I wanted to be part of it again so badly that I was terrified the reality wouldn't live up to my expectations."

"But it did?" Tony asked.

"Sometimes it did. Sometimes it didn't. But the fact that it was real—that I knew it wasn't just some kind of machine magic—well, that made everything . . . I don't know. Count more, I suppose. Does that make sense to you? It made me want to *really* see all the places I'd visited only through Peter's computer programs."

"Well, then, maybe you'll come with me when I go to the real Bar Passatempo," Tony suggested. "Now that you're free to explore, and Peter doesn't need you as much as he once did."

Rita's expression was happy and sad at the same time. "My little beast," she said quietly. "He and Bonnie are going to have the most incredible journey. . . ."

Peter and Bonnie danced on the sun-washed deck of a boat, sailing off on a worldwide adventure. The gray-blue ocean was all around them. Nothing but water as far as they could see. Her skin was warm, and she smelled as sweet and fresh as honeysuckle on the wind.

"This was the way it always was in my daydreams," Peter whispered to her.

"Well, you don't have to imagine any longer," Bonnie whispered back. "And neither do I."

They swayed in perfect rhythm, their music the swish of gentle waves against the hull, the cries of the freewheeling gulls, and the beating of their own hearts.

Lying forgotten on the floor of Bonnie's father's truck, a shriveled, dried-up rose was all that was left of the beast.